DON'T JUDGE A DUKE BY HIS COVER

Dukes in Danger
Book 1

Emily E K Murdoch

DRAGONBLADE PUBLISHING, INC.

ARE YOU SIGNED UP FOR DRAGONBLADE'S BLOG?

You'll get the latest news and information on exclusive giveaways, exclusive excerpts, coming releases, sales, free books, cover reveals and more.

Check out our complete list of authors, too!

No spam, no junk. That's a promise!

Sign Up Here

www.dragonbladepublishing.com

Dearest Reader;

Thank you for your support of a small press. At Dragonblade Publishing, we strive to bring you the highest quality Historical Romance from some of the best authors in the business. Without your support, there is no 'us', so we sincerely hope you adore these stories and find some new favorite authors along the way.

Happy Reading!

CEO, Dragonblade Publishing

Additional Dragonblade books by Author Emily E K Murdoch

Dukes in Danger Series
Don't Judge a Duke by His Cover (Book 1)

Twelve Days of Christmas
Twelve Drummers Drumming
Eleven Pipers Piping
Ten Lords a Leaping
Nine Ladies Dancing
Eight Maids a Milking
Seven Swans a Swimming
Six Geese a Laying
Five Gold Rings
Four Calling Birds
Three French Hens
Two Turtle Doves
A Partridge in a Pear Tree

The De Petras Saga
The Misplaced Husband (Book 1)
The Impoverished Dowry (Book 2)
The Contrary Debutante (Book 3)
The Determined Mistress (Book 4)
The Convenient Engagement (Book 5)

The Governess Bureau Series
A Governess of Great Talents (Book 1)
A Governess of Discretion (Book 2)
A Governess of Many Languages (Book 3)
A Governess of Prodigious Skill (Book 4)

CHAPTER ONE

January 5, 1810

L AWRENCE KNEW HE would have to hit the man eventually, but it would be so much easier if he could just stay still.

"That was a close one!"

"Come on, Lawrence!"

"Get him!"

The cheers and shouts round the boxing ring rose in a rush of heat and noise, clouding Lawrence's judgment and making it almost impossible to think—at least, it would have done.

If he were a lesser man. If it was not vitally important he—

Lawrence lurched to the side, just missing an errant fist flying in his direction. His opponent grinned, blood oozing from his nose.

The ring was splattered with blood, but as far as Lawrence could make out, most was not his. Not that he'd managed to land many hits, his damned mind otherwise occupied.

He had to find him.

Lawrence circled slowly around the ring. *Ring.* One would hardly call it a ring if any of the men clamoring in the stands had seen where he had learned to box Oxford.

But here in the backstreets of London, the Almonry, any old square would do as long as there was sufficient rope around it, Lawrence thought darkly.

No one required more, nor required names when a man stepped into the ring.

They certainly did not check name given was true...

"Careful!"

A shout from the crowd made him turn and just miss a thrust to his chest, which would have been most injurious to his overall health—and his purpose.

For Lawrence Madgwick had not come to the Almonry Den Boxing Ring to win a little coin, though it would be most useful.

He was not even Lawrence Madgwick at all.

"Ready to give up?" he taunted his opponent, wiping sweat from his eyes in an attempt to ensure he could see the damned man clearly.

He had watched the brute time and time again, could predict the careless way he moved, but for some reason it was far more difficult in the ring.

The man leered. "Tired, old man?"

Now that was most irregular, thought Lawrence. He was barely just thirty.

Though, of course, in the streets of London where anything could happen, perhaps it was an achievement to reach such an old age.

"Never," Lawrence said, twisting as he lunged, a fist aiming for the man's head.

He missed.

It did not matter. The crowd cheered, a hundred or so people gathered to see the match, utterly captivated by the bout.

Heart pounding, Lawrence attempted to remember that he had, after all, volunteered for this. He had known how difficult the work would be, how taxing on a man's body.

But he had never expected his bones to ache this badly, or for his chest to cry out that there must be a better way to find the blighter.

"Come on, Lawrence!"

Lawrence glanced round. The face he had been searching for was not there, he was certain. Prolonging the fight, pretending he had nothing better to do than accept the brute's punches, was wearisome but necessary.

And now he was sure the blaggard was not in the crowd. That meant it was time to end this particular fight.

Tensing his shoulders and moving to the balls of his feet for better balance, Lawrence suddenly charged toward his opponent. A complex set of punches layered with a twist of his chest to prevent retaliatory strikes from landing, Lawrence felt no pleasure, only frustration, as his opponent fell to the ground, clutching at his jaw.

The crowd erupted. Rising to their feet, cheering and stamping, the crowd gave adulation that Lawrence, if he had truly been a boxer, would have adored.

But he was not.

Hand lifted into the air by the referee, a wrinkled old man called Fred, Lawrence bowed his head graciously to accept the praise.

"Outstanding bout!"

"Good on you, man!"

"—never saw such a spectacular fall—"

Lawrence ignored the cries as he stepped out the ring and approached the man who had, for the last six months, pretended to be his boxing coach.

"Still no sign of him?" muttered Alan.

Lawrence shook his head, accepting the cloth offered and wiping his brow. "I would have thought by now the blaggard would have returned."

"Anything can keep a man in France if there is enough coin to it," said Alan heavily, glancing round the place. "You know that."

Lawrence sighed. *He did indeed.*

Nothing he experienced at Oxford could have prepared him for the work he had slipped into once leaving its halls. Nothing could have helped understand the sacrifices he would make.

Six months in London, in the worst part of town, far from his home and the comforts it offered…

After all, the Duke of Penshaw had a rather sizeable fortune.

"Time to go."

Lawrence looked up. "I beg your pardon?"

Alan shrugged, his dark though graying hair thinning at the front, which became all the more obvious as he pushed it back. "He's not here. We'll come back tomorrow, hope—"

"The evening is still young," said Lawrence urgently, heart still pounding as panic rose in his chest.

They could not give up, they must continue searching—had they not dedicated enough time on this important task?

"He's not here," Alan repeated under his breath as Fred approached. "You need to rest, regain your strength if you are to fight tomorrow—"

"Fight tomorrow? Why not fight now?" asked Fred with a cheerful grin, slapping Lawrence on the back. "You're not done for, are you?"

Lawrence hesitated. It was true, he could probably fight another bout, though his legs were crying out for relief. *Just five minutes to sit down and gather sufficient thoughts to decide—*

"And there's another half a crown in it for you, m'boy," added Fred as though half a crown would make any difference to a duke.

Lawrence swallowed. *Not that anyone here save Alan knew he was a duke, that was—and it had to stay that way.* It was imperative, if they were ever to track down the blighter who had absconded with government secrets, that no one suspected one of the prize fighters in the Almonry Den had been born to nobler things.

Yet what was nobler than serving one's country?

"I think the boy's had enough," Alan was saying.

Bitter irritation rose in Lawrence's throat. *Six months, he had done what he was told.* Six months they had spent in this awful place, slowly earning his way up through the boxing backstreets.

Six months waiting for the man they knew frequented this place to return.

He was not going to return home like a fool just because he was tired. *Why, the blasted man was likely to turn up at any moment.* What if they missed him merely because he retried for the night?

"No."

Both older men turned to him.

"No?" repeated Alan, a frown on his face.

Lawrence swallowed. He had no wish to upset the man—goodness knows, he had done more than enough in teaching Lawrence to blend with the rabble when his ducal upbringing may have revealed them in a moment—but that did not mean he could order him around.

He was the one who had volunteered for this, he was the one getting his face crushed with each passing day. He was the one whose brother...

"One more bout," he said to Fred, grasping Alan's arm to prevent the man from protesting. "Then home."

A wide smile cracked the face of the referee. "That's m'boy! I've got a special opponent for you, you won't be disappointed—and neither will they."

His hand stretched out at the crowd, clearly eagerly anticipating another fight.

Alan sighed heavily as Fred left them. "You'll wear yourself out."

"I know what I am doing."

"I did not say you did not," he said quietly. "But you'll never replace him, you know. Finding the blaggard who—"

"I said one more bout, Alan, and then home," Lawrence interrupted him, heart skipping a beat painfully. He would not hear his brother spoken of, however obliquely. "I am here for one purpose and one purpose alone, and that is to bring that man to justice. Nothing else. Nothing will distract me, I promise you. We are close. I can feel it."

He held the older man's gaze for a moment, certain they were doing the right thing. *Could he not see?*

His cover as Lawrence Madgwick would only last so long. Eventually someone from the *ton* would come here, scandalous as that would be, and the Duke of Penshaw, who everyone believed was on the Continent, would be recognized.

And that would be the end of it. Their chance to find him.

Alan sighed heavily. "I just hope you don't regret it. I'm going home, my old bones can't take much more of this."

Lawrence nodded silently as he watched the old man push past the crowd to the door.

It had been almost impossible these last few days to think of any reason why he should suffer much more punishment. He longed for his return to Society; even a conversation with Lady Romeril would be preferable to the rabble here, and that was saying something.

He smiled wryly to himself. *Lord, if he was missing Lady Romeril's company, he truly was in trouble.*

One more bout, then. For tonight.

By the time Lawrence reached the ring, there was already someone inside it. Someone huge.

Lawrence swallowed. The man must be half a head taller than him and almost twice as wide. His shoulders twisted with knotted muscles, and a grin revealed the man had lost several teeth.

"Ready?"

Fred was grinning at the side of the ring. A special opponent, that's what the referee had called him.

Damn, the man was almost a mountain! How was anyone supposed to—

"Ready," grunted his new opponent.

Trying to keep his jaw tight, he nodded. *Well, it was his own fault.* He should have listened to Alan, should have realized that there would be nothing good happening this late in the evening. Why, it must be almost midnight.

But he had made his bed, and now he had to lie in it.

And, he thought dryly, *he was most likely to end up lying on his back at the end of this bout.* No man alive, surely, could defeat such a man!

"Ready," Lawrence said.

A cheer went up around the place as Fred stepped out of the ring toward the bell.

Lawrence tried as best he could through exhausted eyes to look along the benches of spectators. The men there—there would be nothing so scandalous as a lady present—were grinning, all eager to see more blood spilled.

Like a gladiatorial ring, Lawrence could not help thinking with a wry smile. Damnation, to think he spent all that time at university studying the classics, yet here he was, getting closer to Roman culture with his fists than he ever had through a book.

Many of the spectators were clutching scraps of paper. Lawrence had to hope they had not bet on him.

The bell rang. The man lunged.

"Come on, Bill!"

Lawrence quickly sidestepped the man, who could more accurately be described as a raging bull, and tried to think. *The man was big, heavy, yes? So he should—*

A heavy punch hit the side of his face, and Lawrence moaned, staggering in an attempt to keep his balance. *Oh, this was a disaster, this was—*

Another punch landed on his stomach, threatening to return his luncheon, not that he'd been able to afford much. To think, when he lived as a duke, there was nothing he could not have on his table. Now he lived off scraps he could barely afford from the pittance he earned here. It was a wonder anyone managed to survive.

His cover would be blown at any moment, Lawrence knew that. It would not be long before someone spotted him, connected the tall, dark man with the duke who had been so eagerly anticipated at the beginning of the Season.

And once his cover was gone—

"The side, hit him in the side!"

He would much rather the brute did not hit him in the side, but it appeared he had little choice. Lawrence attempted to shift his feet, unwilling to move so rapidly, and there was nothing he could do to prevent—

"Ahh!"

Lawrence had not intended to cry out, but the man was immense. Stars erupted in his vision as the place swam, people merging and colliding. When it finally resolved—

A face.

Lawrence blinked, trying to see clearly, trying to think through the cheering, jeering, shouts of encouragement and boos from those who had bet against him. His head was spinning and his heart was only slightly sure of what he had seen.

He blinked again, and the crowd came back into focus. One face in that crowd stood out from all the rest.

A woman.

He must be dreaming. Perhaps the knock to the head had caused more damage than he had thought, for it was unbelievable that a woman—

But she was certainly a woman. There was no mistaking the cut of a gown, the delicate bonnet, eyes wide and mouth moving in words Lawrence could not hear.

She was…beautiful.

She was a distraction, Lawrence tried to tell himself as he staggered around the ring in his attempt to avoid the thrusting punches of his opponent.

Not just a distraction from this damned fight he most certainly should not have accepted—Alan had been right, but when was he ever wrong?—but a distraction from his purpose.

He was here to find John Mortimer.

Lawrence blinked. The woman was looking at him, still shouting something he could not hear amongst the chaotic clamors. Her eyes were bright, her face full of concern.

Concern for him.

A most strange yet not unpleasant lurch twisted his stomach. *What was she doing here?* A boxing ring in the Almonry Den was no place for a lady.

But it was no place for a duke either, and here he was, ostensibly fighting for his life if this swine had his way with him.

Oh, if only they had met elsewhere. If only he had walked past her while promenading on Rotten Row, across a ballroom, at one of Lady Romeril's dratted card parties.

Then he would have been able to introduce himself with his real name, his title. He could have charmed her so utterly, she would have been crying out for his touch by the end of the evening.

His gaze caught hers, and a rush of desire, the like he had never known, overwhelmed him. To think, all he had to do was wait until the end of the fight and—

Pain. Lights, bright lights. Darkness.

Lawrence was in a great amount of pain, which was strange, because he surely had no body. That he did have one, and every inch hurt, suddenly rushed into his understanding as he shifted from unconsciousness.

"Hell's bells!"

He had breathed the words; there had been little enough breath in his chest to say much more.

He was lying on the floor of the ring. He could feel the sawdust. There appeared to be a horse stamping on his head.

Lawrence blinked. No horse, but the pain was real. There was little noise, as though the crowd had gone and left him to his own misery. *Where was Alan?*

A face appeared above his own, one full of concern.

"Alan," Lawrence breathed.

But not Alan. When he blinked again, trying to concentrate on what was above him, he realized Alan was not that young. Nor that pretty.

Lawrence's stomach lurched, and the beautiful woman who had been such a delicious distraction came into focus.

"Sorry," said the woman with a repressed laugh, a mischievous grin across her face that only enhanced the beauty that had been his downfall. "Did I distract you?"

CHAPTER TWO

"*SORRY. DID I distract you?*"

It was all Julia Dryden could do not to laugh, and it was not a laughing matter.

At least, it probably wasn't. The punch that had floored the handsome man so entirely out of his depth had been a harsh one. She wasn't surprised he had fallen to the ground, motionless.

A cheer had risen up the moment he had fallen, half the crowd delighted to see Bill knock another one out, the other half disappointed their wild bets hadn't paid off.

"What a brute," Donald had said, shaking his head.

Julia had leaned forward, eager to see what was going to happen next, pulse throbbing in her ears.

She could never have imagined this. Imagined the noise, the laughter, the shouts, the cries, the chatter as men watched heroes battle before them. Imagined the smells, straw, greasy meat pies, and ale slopped onto the boards as spectators cried out the names of their favorite fighters.

But the sensation Julia was transfixed by was a man. One man.

Only minutes ago, a tall, dark gentleman with a slightly bruised arm and a defiant look had stepped into the ring with that absolute brute of a champion.

"He's a fool," muttered her brother.

Julia nudged him. "And you're a fool for bringing me, you know."

She had meant it as a tease to make the frown on her brother's face disappear—but she realized she had said the wrong thing the moment he caught her eye.

"You're right," said Donald ruefully. "It was a mistake to allow myself to be persuaded, Julia. Ladies should not—"

"I am tired of hearing any phrase that begins 'ladies should not,'" she said curtly with a deepening frown. "Don't be such a bore, Donald."

"I am not a bore! I—"

"There they go," Julia said eagerly, turning to the ring.

She shouldn't chastise her brother really, she had been the one to insist. It was so much more fun, now her brother was of age and could gad about town. Now he could invite her to places Julia was not supposed to be.

This was their first adventure. He had been against it, of course, but had been unable to give five succinct reasons why ladies should not view boxing matches, and so Julia had won.

Her stomach swooped painfully as she watched the two men circle each other in the ring, inspecting for weakness, she supposed.

Goodness, it was thrilling. Why had she never expected such drama, such excitement? True, they were hardly surrounded by people of good name nor standing in Society…

"Punch 'is lights out!" yelled the man seated to her left, throwing a hand in the air, the remnants of the pie he had been eating flying. "G'on Bill!"

Julia looked at him inquisitively. That was the trouble with being born into a family where no one did anything interesting, went nowhere, saw no one save the children of those their mother had been to finishing school with, was forced to smile politely at every Society function.

There was a whole world out there, she had tried to explain to her mother only that morning. A world full of people and things and—

"Oooh!" The crowd gasped as the slighter man, the tall, darker one was punched quite heartily in the chest.

Julia flinched. Her heart beat quickly, stirred by the excitement in the air.

"We should have made a bet," she muttered to her brother.

Donald snorted. "You don't think we've done enough today to scandalize Society if we were caught?"

Julia grinned. "You don't think we've done enough then? I am sure you could always take me to a gaming hell after—"

Her brother rolled his eyes. "Remind me again why I've permitted you to come here."

"Because I wouldn't take no for an answer, that's why," she said happily as the crowd jeered the tall man who appeared to be greatly outmatched. "And because I always get my way."

Donald snorted, but his gaze did not shift from the ring, and Julia turned to it, half expecting to see the tall, dark man on the ground.

But he wasn't. He was trying to do something clever, she could see that. Even a few hours into her first ever night of boxing, Julia had spotted that those quickest on their feet were most likely to stay upright, even if their punches were inadequate.

All he had to do was stay on his feet…

Julia clenched her hands together in her lap, suddenly desperate for the tall man—surely the underdog—to win. There was something about him, even from this distance. Something that told her he was a good man, though precisely how she knew, she was unsure.

Something in his air, his bearing. The way his eyes flashed with intelligence as he attempted to discover a way through the brute's defenses.

"Be careful!" Julia found herself crying out. "Be careful!"

"Julia!" hissed her brother, grabbing her hand as she waved. "What are you—"

"Be—oh, God!"

Her speech ended in a scream as the tall, dark man looked over at her.

Their eyes met.

All sound diminished. All sense of being in a place with near a hundred others faded. All understanding that she was not alone with this handsome stranger disappeared, until all Julia could do was stare.

How was it possible that across a crowded room, seated several yards away as he stood in a boxing ring, blood dripping from his hands, she felt closer to him than anyone she had ever seen?

Her stomach twisted, the world spun, and—

"No!" Julia shouted, along with several others.

The brute had punched the tall man so hard that he fell to the boxing ring floor. Around them, upset mutterings and moans about dodgy betting echoed.

Somehow Julia found herself on her feet.

"Julia, what do you think you're—"

"He'll be alright, won't he?" she said in a tremulous voice.

It was so strange, as though she had known the man for years and had come specially to see him. As though her decision to come here tonight—well, to coerce her brother into taking her—had all been for him.

"He'll be fine," Donald said. "Half of it's for show, I am sure."

Julia bit her lip. It did not look for show, at least from here. The brute, Bill or whatever his name was, was laughing as he stepped around the ring, accepting the crowd's applause. The man on the ground was not moving.

Panic, a sensation she was ill-accustomed to, rushed through her.

"But they aren't doing anything," she said in an anxious voice.

Donald waved a hand airily. "They know what they're doing."

"But we've got to—"

"We've got to go home, Julia," her brother said firmly, pulling a pocket watch from his waistcoat and shaking his head. "Lord, if

Mother discovers you are out of bed—"

"But what about—"

"Julia!"

Julia looked into her brother's face. It did not matter that she was a year older. He was the man of the house, and that made her his responsibility.

"We need to go home," he repeated seriously. "It was scandalous to even think of bringing you here, let alone actually doing it. The best we can hope for now is that we can slip into the house with no one noticing."

Any other day, Julia would have nodded. After all, it was rebellious of her to be here. She had seen no other woman in the crowd, other than...

Her cheeks burned. *Well. That sort of woman.*

And her brother had been kind to bring her, understanding when she had put her foot down and insisted she wanted to see more of the world than what ladies were permitted.

But she could not just leave him there.

The thought rushed through her mind in a crowd of worry for the man she had never spoken to. It was ridiculous, foolish. She had never believed in love at first sight until—

Not that she did now.

Julia cleared her throat. "I just want to ensure he's unharmed."

"Unharmed?" Donald was staring incredulously as the crowd started to dissipate. There were clearly no more fights that evening. "Julia, he's lying on the ground unconscious!"

"All the more reason to ensure he will live," she said firmly.

Where were these words coming from? She had no idea, just the absolute certainty she needed to go down and see him. Protect him. Ensure he was...

She couldn't understand it herself, let alone explain it to her overprotective younger brother.

"You go home," Julia said resolutely, not taking her eyes from the prone figure below them. "I'm—"

"You are absolutely not going down there," said Donald emphatically.

Julia grinned, though her heart still pattered painfully. "Remind me, when did you last instruct me to do or not do anything and I obeyed?"

Her brother groaned, but she did not remain in her seat to hear his argument. Stepping lightly down the steps, avoiding the remnants of food, spilled beer, and what appeared to be gamblers notes evidently not worth anything, Julia fixed her eyes on the ring before her.

It was larger than she had expected. From a distance, the ring had seemed tiny, and she had wondered how the two men had managed to go around and around in such extravagant circles.

No longer.

Julia stared up at the ropes stained with blood. Her heart skipped a beat as she saw the prone figure on the ground.

"Julia, no!"

Happily ignoring the cry of her brother, Julia found the steps into the ring and ducked under the rope.

Most of the crowd was gone now. The noise that had filled the place for hours had dissipated, and Julia discovered her breath was the loudest thing she could hear.

She knelt by the man and, heart in her mouth, leaned over him.

He was, without a shadow of a doubt, a handsome man. Dark, wavy hair crowded his forehead as he lay there, a trickle of blood drying on the side of his temple. A passionate mouth, a frame that appeared more due a nobleman than a common fighter, and hands that...

Julia swallowed. *No. It was most uncouth of her to even think that. She wouldn't.*

She gasped. The man below stirred, moving his head slightly as though checking it was still attached to his neck. His eyes blearily opened, revealing dark green pupils.

He blinked, and her stomach lurched.

"Alan?"

It was all Julia could do not to laugh. *This was ridiculous!* She was not even supposed to be here, and now she was kneeling in the boxing ring over a fighter who had the wind knocked out of him.

What would her mother say!

"Sorry. Did I distract you?" she said brightly, hoping to goodness he would continue to look at her.

Far more tantalizing this close.

He blinked, then suddenly seemed to realize where he was. He launched himself upward, trying to stand, but collapsed into her arms the moment he became vertical.

"Steady, man," Julia said, lowering him slowly into her lap and trying not to think how wonderful those firm fingers felt on her arms. "You've had a terrible fall."

The man blinked. "I—I...who are you?"

"She's trouble, that's what she is," said a rueful voice.

Julia glared at her brother, standing just outside the ring. "I don't need your nonsense, Donald!"

"Julia, we need to *go*," he said urgently, widening his eyes as he emphasized his point. "*Now!*"

But Julia couldn't leave him. The man on the ground was still nestled in her arms, leaning against her as though she could protect him from the world. A strange sort of protectiveness overwhelmed her heart.

She wouldn't leave...what was his name?

"What's your name, sir?" she asked urgently.

The man hesitated. *Goodness,* Julia thought wildly, *he must have been hit hard, if he is having to consider that!*

"Lawrence," he said quietly. "Lawrence Madgwick."

Delight rushed through Julia, a delight she knew was most rebellious, but she could not help it.

She was in a boxing ring, clutching a man to her chest who evidently was of working class stock, and she was on first name terms with him. *First names!*

"I'm Julia," she said firmly. "And—"

"Julia!"

"Go away, Donald," Julia said happily.

The man could have been anyone, yet it was *him*. Lawrence. A sense that her whole life had been roaring toward this point was settling in her soul, and Julia could not shake it off.

"Julia?" Lawrence repeated.

And only then did he seem to realize where he was—more precisely, that he was clasped to Julia's—

"Thank you, I am sure," he said stiffly, pulling himself out of her grasp. "But I really can—"

"You can't," said Julia hurriedly, standing up and wondering why on earth her breath was so tight in her lungs. "You have had a great knock, you simply cannot return—"

"I am quite well, I assure you," Lawrence said with a brief smile. "Thank you."

Julia stood, gown covered in wood shavings from the boxing ring floor, her hands somehow bereft now she was no longer holding onto him, a dizziness in her head she could barely control.

She wanted to be near to him.

The thought rushed through her mind, slipping past her defenses and burrowing its way into her heart, and she could not pull it out.

Because though there was absolutely no reason why she should feel this way, Julia knew she had to be with him. Knew stepping away from Lawrence Madge, or whatever his name was, would be a mistake.

The greater mistake, she tried to tell herself, *was staying here.* She may not have a fancy title, but she was an elegant member of Society, whereas this Lawrence was evidently nothing of the sort.

Perhaps that was why he intrigued her so much.

"I thank you, Mrs...." Lawrence raised an eyebrow.

Julia's heart skipped a beat. He was devastatingly handsome, so much so she hardly noticed the error. "Dryden."

"I thank you, Mrs. Dryden, for your kind attentions," he continued in a stiff voice. "You can go now."

"Thank heavens, some common sense," came Donald's words. "Julia, we need to—"

"You go on home, Donald, I'll see you for breakfast tomorrow," Julia found herself saying. "Go on. I'll be perfectly safe."

She had not taken her eyes from Lawrence. *How could she?* Every moment in his presence was something precious, though she could not for the life of her understand why.

Pulling her pelisse closer, Julia barely registered her brother's muttered oaths as he left her alone with Lawrence.

He was looking at her most peculiarly, and Julia had to admit, it was pleasant to be looked at by such a man. "Your husband is right. You should leave with him."

Julia laughed, her merriment echoing now around the empty hall. "Hus—oh, you mean Donald."

Lawrence nodded, wiping his brow with the back of his hand. "You are fortunate, Mrs. Dryden, that—"

"Oh, he's not my husband," Julia said as airily as she could manage.

If only her heart was not pounding so painfully. She could never have imagined she would find herself in such a precarious position, but here she was.

Alone. At night. In the dark. With a handsome man who was evidently of no respectable family but had the looks of a devil about him. A charming one.

Something shivered up her spine.

"Oh." Lawrence smiled. "Oh. Good. I mean—"

"But I suppose you will wish to return to your wife," Julia said, realization suddenly dawning.

Because it would be too splendid, wouldn't it, for such a man as Lawrence to be unmarried. One only had to look at him to know the ladies would fawn over such a man.

She would be. She was.

Oh, drat, she was entirely losing her composure!

"I am, sadly, unmarried," said Lawrence quietly.

Julia could not help a flush tinging her cheeks. *Was he laughing at her?* A part of her did not care if he was. A man like that could laugh at her all day long, if only she could be near him.

What had got into her? No such thoughts had ever touched her heart like this before. But then, Julia had never met a man like him. Broad and overwhelmingly handsome, and looking at her now in a way she rather liked, yet knew at the same time he certainly should not be.

Curiosity curled around her heart. "Have you boxed for long?"

"I really shouldn't be talking to you," said Lawrence stiffly. "Not without a chaperone."

Julia's cheeks darkened. "I would not have thought a man like you would have cared about such things."

The words slipped out before she could stop them, and she regretted them immediately.

Lawrence's brow darkened. "A man like me?"

"I just meant—"

"A common man, a working class man, a man who earns his bread with his hands, is that it?" he said angrily.

Julia bit her lip. That was what she had meant, but not in the vicious way he intoned.

"I...I have never met anyone like you," she breathed.

The floor seemed to be moving, for the world was spinning and the only thing staying still was Lawrence.

He had stepped closer, closing the gap. Julia breathed in his scent of musk and power and passion.

"I'll put you in a carriage," Lawrence said darkly. "And you'll never see me again, you hear?"

Julia jutted out her chin as the uncouth man grabbed her elbow and started pulling her to the door. She did not resist him—she really should be getting home, in all honesty, for if her mother was to discover she was missing from her bed…

But she was not about to take such directions lying down.

"I'll get in a carriage and go home," she said boldly, hardly knowing where the bravery came from for such a sentence, "but you'll be seeing me again."

CHAPTER THREE

January 7, 1810

L AWRENCE WINCED. "NOT so hard!"

"Oh, I'm sorry, did you want me to fix this cut a little more gently?" asked Alan in a growl. "Then perhaps you shouldn't have allowed yourself to get utterly—"

"Yes, yes, I know," Lawrence said hastily, raising up a bandaged hand.

His digs in Endell Street were only just large enough for two people, but it had been impossible to clean the cut on the back of his head properly.

Another souvenir gained after staying late in the boxing ring without his boxing coach. Another mistake.

And another night, he thought privately, *Miss Julia Dryden had not appeared.*

Not that he had been looking for her. Obviously. No matter what Lawrence might want, the place was far too dangerous for a lady, let alone one that beautiful.

"Stay still!"

Lawrence raised both hands in mock surrender as his friend gently dabbed at the cut with fresh cotton. It stung, but not as much as his twofold disappointment.

Firstly, that the blaggard John Mortimer had still not returned to the Almonry Den. It was outrageous. No one had ever said to Lawrence that he would have to stay here for weeks, let alone months.

"You could always return home," murmured Alan, as though able to see into his mind.

Lawrence's jaw tightened. "And admit defeat?"

"You're getting defeated plenty enough in the ring," Alan pointed out. "Why not go back to Penshaw, be the duke again, live in fine—"

"Because that bastard killed my brother," Lawrence spat, trying to keep still to prevent the searing pain from rushing through his neck. "You know that. When he stole those secrets from my brother, killing him in the process, I made a promise. And I don't back down from a fight."

He could hear rather than see Alan shake his head and sigh, but he knew the man agreed with him. Neither of them would permit John Mortimer to return to England and return to his old tricks of murder and treason.

Besides, returning home to the safety and seclusion of Penshaw up in the north had been a tantalizing offering just a few days ago. Something he had thought dreamily about in the early hours of the morning when he returned to his digs, another day wasted.

It *had* been.

Now his thoughts were otherwise engaged, with the face of a beautiful woman…

"We only guessed he would be coming back to the Almonry Den."

Lawrence sighed heavily. He could not deny Alan's words, but that did not mean he had to like them. "I know."

"And no one has recognized you?"

It was an important question. In fact, it had been Lawrence's first concern when he had agreed to put his boxing skills to the test and slip undercover in the murky world of London's fighting class.

The whole cover would be blown if someone from the gentry

decided to lower themselves for an evening and spotted the notorious Duke of Penshaw in the ring.

Lawrence shook his head as Alan stepped around him. "No, I do not think so."

Though he spoke the truth, a strange twist enveloped his stomach.

Well, Miss Dryden and her brother were gentry, it was true. That had surprised him, seeing two people of quality there, but he was not wrong. Lawrence could recognize the signs of good breeding from a hundred paces, and the two of them were well-to-do, even if they had no titles to speak of.

Yet they had not recognized him.

Lawrence blew out a heavy breath. *At least, they had not said anything.* There had been no glint of recognition in her eyes; that was surely the reason he had looked into them so deeply...

"Lawrence?"

He started. Alan had clicked his fingers before the duke, a wry grin on his face.

"That's Penshaw to you," jested Lawrence, ignoring the momentary loss of concentration.

It had been a point of debate between them when they had first met. Lawrence had stiffly requested that when alone, he would be addressed as Penshaw. A compromise, he had thought. Not so formal as "Your Grace," but not so familiar as to astound anyone.

After six months, it hardly mattered.

"Mr. Penshaw," Alan said, eyes twinkling. "I'm off."

"Off?" Lawrence repeated. Had he missed part of the conversation? Had the memories of Julia—of Miss Dryden—distracted him that much?

A woman with those features was likely distracting people everywhere she went...

Alan clicked his fingers again. "Damnit man, how hard were you hit yesterday?"

Lawrence sighed. "Hard enough to know better. Go on with you, spend your afternoon as you will. I'll see you this evening."

"Six o'clock sharp," his boxing coach warned with a wagging finger. "I don't want to have to apologize any longer for your tardiness!"

It was all Lawrence could do not to laugh. "I'll make a note."

The digs were quiet after Alan shut the door behind him. *Well, digs.* Lawrence snorted. He could never have imagined before he had taken on this assignment, that anyone could survive in such measly accommodation.

Two rooms. One he had turned into his bedchamber, the room just large enough to fit a single bed, the other a mixture of parlor, kitchen, and drawing room.

Lawrence sighed heavily and leaned back in the armchair he had managed to buy for a shilling. The stuffing was partly gone on one side, but the embroidery had kept the rest intact. It was far more comfortable than the wooden chair he had found in the rooms when he had taken them.

To think, his butler's chambers were more luxurious than this!

A prickle of nostalgia crept into his heart. Though he tried to push it away, it overwhelmed him. *Penshaw Place.* A beautiful manor, hundreds of miles away.

Thank goodness his sister was there to look after it—*although,* Lawrence thought with a start, *she would be in town now, wouldn't she? Here, in London.*

Goodness, the very thought…

At least their paths would not cross. Lawrence groaned as he moved to the window, seeking something to distract him. No, no self-respecting lady would deign to be seen anywhere on Endell Street—

Something caught his eye.

A bonnet. Slightly larger than fashionable, though Lawrence was often behind when it came to women's styles—*why did they have to change so blasted often?*—with a blue ribbon edging it that was remarkably familiar.

25

Familiar? Lawrence blinked. He had seen no ladies of repute for so long, how could it possibly be...

His stomach left his chest, falling past his knees and down to the floor.

Miss Julia Dryden.

It was definitely her. No one else had those sparkling eyes, glittering even from this distance, no one else held themselves like that, proud yet curious.

She was out of her depth. Lawrence's jaw fell open as he watched her serenely stride down the street, no chaperone in sight, then swiftly duck through a doorway and into...

Into the Almonry Den.

Lawrence's temple throbbed. He had taken these rooms for just such a view. Perhaps he would spot Mortimer not from the ring itself, but from his rooms.

But he couldn't just stay here, he told himself frantically as he searched around the room for his coat, while Julia—while Miss Dryden was in there alone. It wasn't safe.

A slow smile crept across his face as he hurried down the stairs out onto the bustling street. She had managed to give her brother the slip, at any rate, which rather endeared her to him.

Not that he should be thinking about such a woman. Not that he should be thinking of any woman.

No, Lawrence told himself as he crossed the street, narrowly missing a cart hellbent on accelerating through a crowd rather than avoiding it. He needed to concentrate. He was a duke in danger here, a spy, a man undercover.

All he needed to think about was—

"Ah, Lawrence," Julia said brightly the moment he stepped into the Almonry Den. "I wondered if I would find you here."

Lawrence swallowed. All words slipped down his gullet.

What could he say?

Sunlight was spearing through the windows—not all still filled with glass—and poured past Julia, illuminating her like an angel. If an angel was wearing a matching pelisse to her bonnet, an umbrella tucked on her arm, and a reticule on the other.

If an angel could have such luxurious hair, escaping her hair pins. If an angel had curves like—

"Lawrence?"

Lawrence blinked. He was starting to make a habit of this lack of attention, and it did not bode well.

Particularly when he would have to step into the ring tonight.

"Julia," he said, then cleared his throat. "I mean, Miss Dryden."

The beaming smile on the woman told Lawrence she was pleased to be addressed by her first name.

It went against his character, all his training. Why, Lawrence had not even known his governess had a first name until he was sent to school and made to sign a letter of thanks his father had drawn up.

Only after asking who Vivienne was did he realize that ladies had more than a surname. Miss Clarke was also a Vivienne. Most unsettling.

But Julia…

Miss Dryden, Lawrence reminded himself. Julia suited her better. Which was a pity, for he would absolutely follow propriety now. No duke would do anything less.

"Miss…" Lawrence hesitated.

Yes, that would be what a duke would do. Yet he was here pretending *not* to be a duke. That was the whole point.

It had never occurred to him before, but only as he stood before the beautiful woman—*not that he was looking*—did Lawrence realize he had been treating this undercover business wrong from the start.

He had seen it as a frustration, a reason to grow bitter, all the rights and privileges due to him, as Duke of Penshaw, stripped away.

But only now did he see that it was quite the opposite.

Why, he was free. Free from rules and restrictions, free to speak his mind, utter an opinion without worrying about whether it would offend.

He could eat pies, drink beer, laugh at bawdy jokes, and call Miss Dryden…

"Julia," Lawrence said with a slow smile. "I was surprised to see you enter the Almonry Den, so took it upon myself to…well. Hello."

"Hello," said Julia, blushing prettily.

Lawrence's mouth went dry. *No, this was ridiculous. He* was no green gilled fool of one and twenty; he was near thirty! Had seen plenty of pretty women in his time, had danced with them, kissed them, bedded a few.

Had their mamas whisper details of dowries that bored him senseless…

But this was different.

Lawrence took an unconscious step toward her, managed to stop himself, then stood there, staring with a faint smile.

This woman was not proposing herself as a potential Duchess of Penshaw. Why, she had no idea who he was, what marriage to him could mean for her.

For perhaps the first time in his life, Lawrence had attracted the attention of a pretty woman simply for being…himself.

It was a heady thought. One that should have told him precisely how much danger he was in. Somehow his reason started slipping through his fingers and all he could do was grin.

"You look well," said Julia, nodding at his injuries.

"What, this?" Lawrence said, glancing at the bandages on his hands and wishing to goodness he had not moved his head so swiftly. "Nothing to concern you."

"Well, I will admit that I was concerned," she said, stepping closer as a pair of men strode behind her toward the ring.

Lawrence's breath caught in his throat. They were but a foot apart now. *God, this was the closest he had been to a woman in six months.* The boxing ring did not attract ladies—in truth, it was scandalous to think even one had traversed through this place.

And of all the ladies in London…it was her.

"I wanted to ensure you were doing well," Julia said quietly.

Lawrence nodded but did not speak. His attention had been distracted by a group of men the other side of the ring. They were muttering, and though he could not hear precisely what they were saying from this distance, their frequent glances over at himself and Julia were enough.

His jaw tightened. He had been instructed not to draw attention to himself, blend in, merely become part of the Almonry Den. That was imperative. Impossible as it was to know if anyone was reporting to Mortimer, the last thing they wanted was for the man to catch wind of something strange. Something to prevent him returning.

And there was nothing more strange than a woman in the Almonry.

"You have to leave," Lawrence said abruptly.

It could not be more evident by the raised eyebrow on Julia's face that she did not think much of that suggestion. "I do?"

Why did those two simple syllables send a rush of something close to desire up his spine?

"You do," he said firmly. "It is not seemly to—"

"Not seemly? Lord you sound like my brother."

Lawrence's hackles rose. For a reason he was not going to investigate right now, his entire body rebelled at the idea of being compared to Julia's brother.

Oh, no. What he wanted to do to her was definitely not brotherly…

"Julia, you must see that—"

"Oh, *must* I?" Julia said with a dry laugh. "You know, I spend my life being told what I must do, must say, whose card parties I simply must attend. I thought here, I could just be at peace for more than five minutes."

There was no pettiness in her tone, no petulance. Just frustration.

Well, he knew the restrictions of a life in Society. Though it was clear he and Julia had never met when living under his true identity, they undoubtedly would have both attended Almack's, forced themselves through the dullest of dinners...

They may even have both survived card parties at Lady Romeril's, which was a badge of honor.

But he could not show her his sympathy, nor reveal how closely he related to her frustrations.

Not if he was going to keep his cover.

"A lady like you, you should be promenading down Rotten Row, riding in Hyde Park," Lawrence said aloud with what he hoped was a nonchalant smile. "Things ladies do."

Julia snorted in a most unladylike manner. "And you are the expert on ladies?"

Lawrence forced down a smile. *If she had any idea who she was speaking to...* "I do, as a matter of fact."

He should not have spoken. Julia's eyes lit up, and somehow all the gruffness in his voice had gone.

"You said a few days ago that you were a common man, a working class man, a man who earns his bread with his hands, did you not?" she said quietly as a shout went up from somewhere. Someone appeared to have dropped something heavy.

Lawrence did not take his eyes from the captivating woman before him.

"We come from different worlds, you and I."

He could quite heartily agree with this, but managed to prevent himself from speaking. It would not do to attract more questions. He was supposed to be here undercover, not attracting attention.

So why did he want to attract Miss Julia Dryden far more than was appropriate?

"You'll be fighting again this evening, I suppose?"

Lawrence nodded, seeing swiftly where this conversation was going. "And you would do well to heed my advice, Julia, and—"

"Jules."

He blinked. A faint flush stained the pretty woman's cheeks, but it was nothing to the blazing heat in her eyes.

Jules? Surely he had misheard. There was no possibility a woman like that would ask what she thought was a rough, common man to call her by such a name.

At least, the rough, common man she thought he was.

"Julia," he said quietly. "I do not think you know what you are doing."

He had meant the words as a kindness.

Fire flashed in her eyes. "I know precisely what I am doing. I may just be a woman, but—"

"I didn't mean it like that," interjected Lawrence hastily. Did this woman always have a penchant for misunderstanding? "I meant, you and I, we are from very different worlds—"

"And yet here you are," she said lightly. "Talking to me."

Lawrence swallowed. Yes, he was, and against his better judgment, too. But there was something about Julia, something that drew him in. It was not possible to walk away from her, no matter how much more sense it would make to do so.

His cover could not be blown. *He was here*, Lawrence reminded himself, *to catch his brother's killer and a traitor to the king's government.*

Not to flirt with pretty young things he wanted to take back to his digs and—

"You interest me, Lawrence."

Lawrence felt a most disconcerting sensation. Heat. On his cheeks. *Dear God, was he blushing?*

"You intrigue me," Julia said in a low voice. "You make me... curious."

He swallowed. "I do not intend to."

"And that is what makes it all the more interesting," she said with a smile. "I have been bored out of my mind in polite Society for far too long, that was why I made Donald take me to the boxing, and then you...you."

The way she spoke, it was so simple. He could almost believe their conversations, their connection could pass unnoticed.

But then a voice from the other side of the boxing ring rose. "—outrageous, the two of them standing there! And her a lady!"

Lawrence's desire was forced down as reason took charge. "I am sorry, Miss Dryden, but I do not have time to be an oddity or your entertainment today," he said coldly. "And I advise you, again, to heed your brother. Do not return to the Almonry Den."

It was all he could do to prevent himself from looking back as he strode away.

CHAPTER FOUR

January 10, 1810

H E REALLY WAS the most disobliging man she had ever met.

Julia sniffed, then immediately wished she hadn't. Though Almack's was not the paragon of perfection, as so many of the ladies in Society pretended, it was at least clean.

The same could not be said for the Almonry Den.

But then, Donald would undoubtedly say that it was her own fault for coming. She hadn't been able to stay away. Three days at the most, then Julia had stained and ruined a perfectly good cushion after losing track of her teacup only that afternoon.

"Oh, Julia, attend!" her mother had scolded, whipping the offending teacup from her hands. "I do not know what has got into you lately, you barely paid any attention to the Dowager Duchess of Chantmarle! Have you forgotten your deadline—you must find a husband by Easter or I—"

"Will find one for me, yes," Julia had been forced to say. Then smile, apologize, and pretend her mind wasn't two miles away, far from the respectable Mayfair, and instead…

Julia smiled nervously at a man sitting down the bench, gawping at her. "Good evening."

The man continued to gawp.

She could not blame him. It *was rare enough for a woman to be here*, thought Julia as the growing crowd's voices started to echo around the large hall. It was even less usual for a woman to be here on her own.

Which she wouldn't be, if not for her disagreeable brother.

"Donald, where are you?" Julia muttered under her breath.

It really was too bad of him. Why, he had agreed only a few hours ago to meet her outside the Almonry Den, and she had waited for near twenty minutes. At least, it had felt like twenty minutes. Despite asking her mother for a pocket watch, or something that would help her tell the time while out and about, her mother's outraged face had been sufficient a reply.

And so she had come inside.

Which had not felt rebellious at the time. *After all,* Julia told herself as the stands started to fill up with no sign of Donald, *it was surely less ladylike than standing outside in the dark as though…*

Well. *As though she were a lady of the night.*

But now she was seated here alone, she started to realize how delicate her situation was.

A woman. A lady, a lady of her social standing… alone. At a boxing ring.

Julia bit her lip. She would not admit her brother had been right, not even if she had to suffer the indignity of being gawped at by all around her.

Anything to have the chance to see—

"I thought you wouldn't heed my advice," said a dry, deep voice. "I don't know why I thought you might."

Julia's stomach curled with delight. There, standing just along the row, with his hands in his coat pockets and a wry smile on his face, was—

"Lawrence," she said, trying to keep the delight firmly from her tones. "Why, I did not think to see you here."

It was a lie, of course.

Try as she might, Julia had not yet plucked up the courage to pay someone—a maid perhaps, or one of the footmen—to discover more about the mysterious Lawrence Madgwick.

Where he went. Where his rooms were, though the very thought of discovering such a thing made shivers rush along her bones. Where he frequented, other than the Almonry Den.

And so, Julia had been *forced* to return here. The only place she could be sure she would see the handsome young boxer.

Never mind he was entirely the wrong sort of person for her to be associating with. Never mind her mother would undoubtedly shriek if she saw the state of his nails.

Never mind she'd had a wild dream last night, filled with the scent of Lawrence, and heat, him saving her from a terrifying thing she could no longer remember now...

No, her memory was crowded only with sensations. Touches.

"Where else would I be?" Lawrence said heavily, sitting beside her on the bench.

Julia swallowed. He was close. *Too close.* Closer than any gentleman, even the few who had wished to gain her affections.

Mr. Lister had been the boldest. He had once sat on the same sofa as her, ignoring her chaperone. At the time, she had thought it outrageous! No man should be that brazen with a lady.

Now Julia wished Lawrence was closer. The fabric of his breeches was touching her gown. Something prickled her skin, making every inch heightened, as though...as though something was going to happen.

"Where's that brother of yours?"

Julia swallowed. It was imperative she give no indication of how rattled she was.

"Donald?"

Lawrence nodded. Julia tried not to look at the way his stubble was starting to meet his sideburns along that sharp jawline.

Tried. It was difficult not to, seated as they were.

She took a deep breath with the intention to reply but was overcome by his scent. *Dear God, she had never smelled a man like this.* All others had been gentlemen, not men of the lower classes. Not men who earned a living with the sweat of their brow.

Lawrence was a man who worked with his hands.

Despite everything she knew a lady should be, Julia glanced at his hands, brought together and resting between his knees.

She swallowed. *Hands she had most definitely dreamed about.* It was all rushing about to her now, the way he had held her—

"Jules?"

Julia smiled weakly. "I like it when you call me Jules."

A sharpness returned to her eyes as she realized what she had just said. *Goodness, if she was not careful, she would start to have a reputation.*

Not that there was a single person at the Almonry Den who would find themselves at Almack's.

Stifling a smile at the thought, she spoke more firmly. "Donald. Yes, I thought he would be here to meet me. He did promise, but I have a terrible feeling his gaming hell has distracted him."

Julia thought, on the whole, she should be congratulated for speaking of her brother's disreputable habits so calmly. Their mother always hushed her voice whenever debts appeared in crisp white envelopes.

But Lawrence did not seem concerned. "You still should not be alone, though. You should return home, back to civilization."

There was a dry wit to his words that made Julia smile. "I'm not alone though, am I? I am with you."

She had not intended to speak so companionably to a man she knew nothing about, a man she had only met above a week ago.

But there was something about this Lawrence Madgwick. Something that settled her spirits yet drove them to distraction at the same time. Something that made her feel safe and right on the edge of adventure.

"Yes, I suppose you are," said Lawrence quietly, the crowd around them roaring as the first two combatants stepped into the boxing ring. "But how do you know you are safe with me?"

Julia shivered. Whether it was the excitement of the crowd, the heady presence of the man beside her, or the remnants of her dream slipping into her mind, she did not know.

Whatever it was, she knew she was absolutely not safe with Lawrence Madgwick.

"I don't," she breathed, her gaze catching his own. "That is what makes it so exciting."

Lawrence said nothing, merely looked at her, as the referee bellowed the names of the two men who had stepped into the ring.

At least, Julia thought that was what he said. She could not tell.

Lawrence. A man she would never have met in the polite drawing rooms she spent her days frequenting, a man who knew what it was to fight and strive and work hard.

Julia swallowed. *She had to be careful.*

A slow smile crept across his handsome features. "You are rebellious, Jules, if you do not mind me saying so."

"And you are bold to say so, which suggests you are just as rebellious as I," Julia said, hardly daring to take another breath.

He laughed. "Bold?"

Julia nodded. She never would have dared to speak in such a way to one of the servants, and she supposed they were the same class as Lawrence.

But then, no one was the same class as Lawrence. He was in a class all of his own.

"I think you are," she said, trying to hold onto her nerves as the fight began and those around them cheered.

Lawrence nodded slowly. "Yes, I suppose I am, though not why you think."

"You take your life into your own hands every time you step into that ring," Julia pointed out.

This was madness. She should not be having a calm conversation with a boxer, in the Almonry Den! She should go home, berate Donald later for refusing to make their rendezvous, and never think of doing something so unruly again.

So why was she almost glued to the bench?

Lawrence laughed dryly. "My life?"

"You're certainly putting it on the line. I heard Donald once talking to our butler about a boxer who lost all his senses after a particularly dangerous fight."

It was the wrong thing to say.

Lawrence raised an eyebrow. "Your butler?"

Julia cursed her lack of thought, but it was too late to take back now. Besides, it was clear as day to anyone by the silk of her gown and her impeccable taste that she came from money, and not just good money, but old money, too.

"My butler," she said, refusing to back down from her position. She forced herself to meet his eyes, though her heart skipped a beat as he smiled. "I am not ashamed of who I am."

"And nor should you be," came his quiet reply. "Still, you must admit you and I come from very different worlds."

There was a teasing smile playing on his lips. Julia found it rather difficult to look away once she had noticed. *They were full, kissable—*

Now where had that thought come from?

"Different worlds, perhaps," she said quietly. "But I imagine we have far more in common than may appear on the surface. Looks can be deceiving."

A cheer went up around them. Julia turned hastily to see that one of the men in the boxing ring had fallen to the ground. There were excited exclamations from a man behind them, who had evidently won a great deal of money.

When she turned back to Lawrence, he was smiling—and this time he did not appear to be teasing.

"You intrigue me almost as much as I think I intrigue you," he said. "And you are right. Looks can be deceiving. I still do not understand why a woman who looks like you decides to spend her evening here, when she undoubtedly has received a good many far better invitations."

The compliment caused heat to rise in Julia's cheeks, though not perhaps the one the handsome man beside her had intended.

Yes, she had plenty of invitations, all stacked along the great marble mantelpiece in the drawing room, some of them gilt edged, some of them with fancy calligraphy, some with impressive titles.

But it was not the recognition that she was a sought after member of the *ton* that had delighted her.

"I still do not understand why a woman who looks like you…"

Looks like her? Why, that had to mean something, did it not?

Strange that a passing compliment the man had evidently not considered meant more to her than all the fripperies thrown at her by wheedling gentlemen at dinners.

"Perhaps I have other places I could be, but I chose to be here."

"Why?" His response was swift, challenging, intrigued.

A flutter of excitement grew in her stomach. *He was interested in her—in her!*

"Because you are nothing like any of the gentlemen I am forced to converse with," Julia found herself saying, words spilling out as the unfortunate soul below them was dragged out of a boxing ring and replaced by another. "Because you make me feel. Feel alive, alive in a way I have never felt before. And I think you feel it, too."

For a moment, she was convinced she had gone too far. Lawrence examined her closely, his dark eyes flashing.

Julia swallowed. *What did she think she was doing, saying such—*

"I have never met a woman who spoke her mind so openly," Lawrence said quietly.

Perhaps it was a coincidence. Perhaps the man on his other side jolted him. But Julia was certain Lawrence had leaned closer, his shoulder brushing up against hers.

A spark of something she was starting to recognize seared through her.

"Truly?" she breathed.

Lawrence nodded. "Why, if I did not have—other things to attend to, I could see myself getting rather distracted by you, Miss Dryden."

Julia had not expected to feel disappointment at such an intimate sentence, but he had not called her Julia.

"Julia, please."

"I prefer Jules, but I—I should not..." Lawrence appeared to lose his tongue for a moment before turning back to the fight and resolutely continuing without looking at her. "How do you like his chances?"

She knew why he had done it, of course. It was not seemly for the two of them to be talking so closely—they had not even been formally introduced!

Julia stifled a smile at the idea of dragging someone like Lawrence Madgwick, in his oft-mended jacket and mismatched waistcoat, to be introduced at Almack's.

The very idea...

"Chances?" she said vaguely, trying to focus on the fight.

From what she could see, the bout was one sided. One of the men looked like the brute who had knocked Lawrence out. The other was a sprightly looking man, all sinew, no muscle.

"Surely it must go one way," Julia said quietly. "I mean, the smaller man cannot possibly win."

"You think so?"

She glanced at Lawrence. There was a knowing smile on his face, one that made her lungs tighten, just for a moment.

"And you don't?"

Lawrence shook his head, lowering his voice and most unaccountably leaning to her.

To ensure that she could hear him, Julia tried to tell herself. But then, why lower his voice in the first place?

"Look at him, really look at him," Lawrence murmured, voice low and full of meaning. "He is underestimated by those around him. People look at him and assume they know all about him—and what's best for him."

Julia's heart was beating frantically now, the intimate nature of their conversation and its scandalous content drawing palpitations and a rush of tenderness.

Oh, this was what she had thought of when she had read about romances, when she had thought what it would be like to sit in the presence of a man one simply could not stay away from—

"And they are wrong?" she breathed.

Lawrence's eyes met hers. There was such intensity there, such devotion, that Julia's lips parted. "Oh, the world thinks it knows best, and he could easily obey, could he not? Only do what he was told, be what they wanted, go only where they said he belonged."

Julia's mouth was dry. "And he won't."

"He won't," said Lawrence with a smile. His hands had somehow moved to his left knee, right beside her own. Tantalizingly near. "That's when you know you've met someone special. When they are told by the world what to do, how to be, who to associate with...and they refuse."

Julia could barely breathe. She was intoxicated with him, what he was saying, who he was. How could he say those words with such calm?

"Those are the sorts of people I wish to know," Lawrence murmured. "That is the type of person I wish to be."

Julia blinked, trying to force reason into her mind, but she could not. *Oh, to be such a person as Lawrence would admire, to see herself through his eyes...*

For was she not such a person? Was this not, in truth, a very clever way of flattering her?

"And is that," Julia whispered, "why you are here? Why you risk everything to find him?"

And all of a sudden, the moment was broken.

She did not know how, did not believe she had said anything to warrant such a change, but in that instant, Lawrence moved away. He leaned back and affixed her with such a sharp look, she felt pinned to the bench.

"What in heavens do you mean by that?" he barked.

Julia stared, utterly at a loss. "I—I just meant, you said you were looking for people like that, to be a person like that, and I thought—if I misunderstood, if I offended—"

"No, no, it's my misunderstanding," Lawrence said hastily, a brief smile creasing his lips, but it was gone again in an instant. "Never you mind."

Another cheer. Another man must have fallen in the boxing ring.

At least, that was what Julia assumed. She had not looked round, unable to drag her attention away from the man who looked unsettled, a wild look in his eyes, a sense of shock not yet dissipating from his features.

What had she said to so disturb him?

"Never mind my mutterings," said Lawrence. "Come, let us focus on what is before us."

Julia swallowed. "Us?"

It was a heady thought. *Us.* Her and Lawrence. A strange sort of courtship, one her mother would certainly not approve—

"The boxing ring," said Lawrence, gesturing at it lazily. "I believe Tom is up next—ah yes, there he is."

Julia's shoulders slumped. She should not have lost herself in imaginings—in remembrances of that ridiculous dream she'd had.

Reality was before her, and that reality was clear. She and Lawrence may meet at the Almonry Den, may marvel at the boxing before them…

But they could not be more different.

CHAPTER FIVE

January 14, 1810

A LTHOUGH HE HAD managed to avoid the temptation for months, it was no longer possible to stay away.

At least, that was what Lawrence told himself.

Just a quick saunter, he promised himself as he slipped out of his digs at Endell Street and meandered to the place in London he had once spent so much time. Just a few moments, to remind himself of where he had come from. What he had sacrificed to be there.

What he would, one day, be returning to.

When Lawrence stepped through the gate by South Carriage Drive, it was such a dazzlingly different scene to what he had become accustomed to the last few months that he halted.

Rotten Row.

A wide track that meandered from Hyde Park Corner, all the way to the Serpentine Road, Rotten Row was absolutely the place to see and be seen. Most people were on horseback, naturally, the upper classes taking the opportunity to exercise their beasts in the chilly winter air. There were many others walking, usually in pairs or small groups. *Plenty of chaperones,* he thought darkly.

"Careful!"

Lawrence stepped aside to see a man attired in gentleman's clothing, a cane in his hand and a pretty lady on his arm.

"Watch where you're going, you lout," said the man coldly.

Lawrence was forced to suppress a smile. He had merely been standing, there was absolutely no possibility he had been in the man's way—but he understood what had happened.

The man had seen him dressed in laborer's clothing, his jacket tatty with no top hat at all, and assumed he should not be there.

And of course, technically, he probably shouldn't.

After all, Rotten Row was for those who could be recognized as nobility and gentry.

Never mind that if Lawrence had been dressed according to his status—in the most impressive greatcoat from George Stulz on Savile Row—the man would have been positively fawning, desperate for his acquaintance...not demanding he step off the path and into the mud merely to satisfy his desire of being perceived as impressive before a lady.

A slow smile crept across Lawrence's face. Odd. When he had been living his life as the Duke of Penshaw, a meander down Rotten Row would not have seemed exciting.

It did now.

"—don't look, my dear, a scoundrel has appeared on the path," came a quiet voice.

Lawrence tried not to smile. He spotted Mr. Lister, a second-class gentleman wearing third class boots, walking with a young lady who seemed most unimpressed with his company.

He bowed deeply, and Mr. Lister sniffed. "The rogue has no idea of manners. Come on, dear, let us avoid the rascal."

Lawrence raised an eyebrow. *Well, if he ever needed evidence that his disguise was working, he had it.* Allowing his stubble to grow and wearing shoddy clothing was evidently all that was required to turn a duke into a mere man.

It was an amusing thought. Why, there were plenty of well-dressed gentlemen walking past him now, each curling their lips at the sight of him—certainly something they would not have done to the Duke of Penshaw.

And there...

Lawrence's heart skipped a beat, something it rarely did. Though now he came to think about it, it seemed to be most disobligingly doing it more often. It was most irritating.

But he could not deny why the discomforting sensation graced his chest.

Miss Julia Dryden.

How had he not spotted her before? There she was, walking sedately alone, which surprised him. Where was that good for nothing brother of hers? Did he always permit her to be so unchaperoned?

Lawrence balked at the idea. Ladies should be accompanied, that was one of the most basic rules of Society...though now he came to think of it, his sister was probably somewhere about, perhaps even here on Rotten Row, without him.

Blast.

The sooner he could find this blaggard and bring him to justice, the better. Every day John Mortimer remained at liberty, Lawrence was forced from his sister, his title, his position—even the grace to walk down Rotten Row without being stared at—and the cad remained free.

It was outrageous.

But for the first time since he had left his life as the duke behind, Lawrence found himself distracted. Julia was a few hundred yards away walking slowly, evidently in no hurry. The instinct to call out to her—Lord above, to call "Julia"—was strong.

Just before his mouth opened, Lawrence managed to stop himself.

To the eyes of the gentry, he was nothing but a scruffy man gawping at his betters.

Which, while untrue, wasn't something he could refute. She had to consider him just another boxer, just another man who fought with his fists, who was nothing better.

The sun peeked out from a cloud, and Julia's chestnut hair lit up.

Lawrence swallowed. Restraining himself had never been this difficult, he'd always had an ironclad control on himself...because he knew precisely what he should do.

Stay away from her.

This was a dangerous business. It was perfectly acceptable for a duke, someone trained in the arts of war, of boxing, who expected the unexpected and looked for danger behind every door.

But for a lady?

No. He would not be the one to encourage Julia to enter a world of murky depths, putting herself in danger. *The idea of her being hurt...*

Lawrence's stomach curdled. It was unthinkable.

But he did not move. Perhaps he had never been tempted like this. Never been tempted by such delicious curves, the light in her eyes, the way her lips...

He cleared his throat, determined to force himself to leave. As he turned around—

"Lawrence! Lawrence, is that you?"

He froze. Julia's eyes had alighted on him, a broad smile on her face as she waved boldly in a manner a lady most certainly should not.

That did not prevent him from smiling in turn. He had never met a woman like her, certainly not a woman in polite Society.

As she strode forward, her pace increasing as she neared him, Lawrence tried to ignore the astonished looks they both were receiving. It was simply not done for a lady to approach a gentleman, even one to whom she had been introduced...but to shout his name across Rotten Row! *His first name!*

Julia's cheeks were pink from the exertion as she reached him. "Goodness, I did not expect to see you here."

Lawrence tried not to smile. There was something so charming about her complete abandon that made her most delightful.

But not, he reminded himself, *delightful enough to endanger her.*

"I know this is hardly the sort of place for a man like me, Jules," he said, trying to restrict the teasing air into his voice.

If only she knew...

Julia grinned. "Rather wild of you, I must say. I am pleased, I am in need of a strong arm."

Before Lawrence could protest, before he could even register what was happening, Julia had slipped her hand into his arm and started walking. He had no choice but to continue, walking in step.

It was as natural as breathing. Perhaps that was why his chest was so tight. Perhaps that was what surprised him the most.

When Lawrence had last been in Town, the *ton* simpering at his every word and following his every step, he had been bored of Society. Bored of the way everyone watched him, adored him, protested that his taste was impeccable and his choices perfection.

If I had no title, he had often thought, *how would they treat me?*

Well, now he knew. As Julia chatted on about why her good for nothing brother had disappointed her once again—*a frequent occurrence, by the sound of it*—Lawrence could not help but notice just how many dirty looks he received merely for walking alongside her.

Yes, she was beautiful. If people had recognized him for the Duke of Penshaw, they would have said, surely, that she was fortunate to be walking with him.

As it was...

"Absolutely shameful," muttered someone as they passed.

"Utterly incomprehensible," said a gentleman, shaking his head.

Lawrence made sure not to catch the eyes of a pair of ladies as they walked by, but he could not prevent hearing their tuts.

"—and I told him—Lawrence, I hate to say it, but you are not listening."

"I beg your pardon?" said Lawrence hastily, looking at the lady on his arm.

Julia was laughing. "My word, I never thought I would hear such formality from you!"

All too late, Lawrence remembered he was supposed to be a man of the working classes, not given to such niceties as "begging pardons" and the politeness of a man of quality.

Which he was. But wasn't.

Lawrence felt a great need to curse under his breath but managed to stop himself. *All this undercover business was mighty difficult.*

"Just trying to speak to you as you deserve," he said stiffly.

Julia rolled her eyes. "Don't start that again—I said I was sorry."

Lawrence nodded with a smile. "And I am not offended—at least, I am not anymore."

He laughed as she turned to him with genuine concern in her eyes, then laughed in relief at his merriment.

"Offended! You! I cannot think what offending you would look like."

As the Duke of Penshaw, almost anything could offend him. At least, offend the title. He had always considered himself a rather easygoing fellow, but it appeared being a duke meant you were supposed to be offended if everything was not immediately to your liking.

It had always felt rather foolish.

"You were the one who pointed out our different stations in life," Lawrence reminded her. "Not I."

Julia sighed happily, her fingers tightening on his arm. Lawrence's stomach gave a lurch. "To think of me, offending you!"

He laughed. "Do not ladies ever give offense?"

"That is a little unfair of you, Lawrence, though I say so myself," she said conversationally as they turned off the end of Rotten Row and started toward some trees.

Lawrence shrugged. "I think it was a little unfair of you to drag me along Rotten Row, where I could be critiqued both silently and openly by those of the *ton*."

He had intended to speak lightly, to jest, to make her smile.

But Julia's face became serious. She was silent for a moment before saying, "Yes, I heard what they said. Isn't it outrageous?"

Now that was not what he had expected. "Outrageous?"

Julia nodded fervently as they stepped closer to the trees, ignoring the damp dewy grass. "I mean, they don't *know* you, do they? All they see is tatty clothes—"

"Why thank you!"

"You know what I mean," she said with a laugh. Lawrence was enchanted to see two little pink dots appear on her cheeks. "My point is, they have spoken nary a word to you and yet assume they know all about you. Why, for all we know, you're a prince in disguise!"

Her tinkling laughter was not accompanied by his own. For a heartbeat, Lawrence was certain she was going to guess; worse, reveal she had known all along that he was a duke and she had merely been having a laugh at his expense.

But evidently, she saw it all as an amusing thing to consider...not the truth. Not quite.

Lawrence forced himself to smile. "Yes, I could be."

Julia giggled as the noise of the crowds disappeared and the trees surrounded them. "Yet, if you were a prince or a gentleman at the very least, you would not have permitted yourself to be alone with me like this. Would you?"

He blinked. *Alone?*

He looked around hurriedly and saw to his genuine surprise that they were completely out of sight. One could just about hear the bustle of the crowd, if one paid attention, but the thickness of the trees, even in winter, had put them in a private world.

And the presence of Julia's hand on his arm suddenly grew in intensity, heating his arm, heating his whole chest.

He was alone with her. A woman he found remarkably desirable, one he had thought about far too much...and here they were. *And she thought him no gentleman...*

"I suppose we are alone," Lawrence said, his voice strangled. "But that is no reason why I cannot treat you like the lady you are."

Julia slipped her hand from his arm, and he almost cried out at the sudden shock of the separation.

How had he become so dependent on her in just a few minutes? How was it possible his whole body ached for her presence, even though she was but a few feet from him?

"Lawrence, you may be good with your fists," said Julia with a teasing smile, "but you wouldn't know what to do with a lady."

And a fire, one he had never known before but roared through him, consumed Lawrence from head to toe. *Didn't know what to do with a lady?*

Oh, how little she knew. How she wished to tease him, to show him just who was in charge here. She was about to discover it...

"Wouldn't know what to do with a lady?" Lawrence repeated.

He stepped forward, closing the gap between them.

Julia's smile disappeared. She did not look frightened, upset, or offended.

No, quite to the contrary. With a groan, he just managed to keep in, he saw desire in her eyes. Desire for what, she evidently did not quite know, but he raised it in her, something that matched the heat within him. Oh, he should not permit himself to be challenged, Lawrence knew, or to be so easily teased into action.

But he had always been like that, hadn't he? Encouraged to act, encouraged to go undercover as a boxer to find his brother's killer.

Encouraged to do something to Julia he most certainly shouldn't...

"Prove it," Julia whispered, her eyes flashing. "Don't give me words, Lawrence. Give me action."

It was no use. Moaning as he pulled the willing woman into his arms, Lawrence crushed his lips on hers and tasted immediately that she wanted it, wanted him.

She had goaded him into this precisely because, as a lady of Society, she was not able to ask for what she wanted.

Julia responded immediately. As Lawrence's hands clasped her waist, drawing her tight into him, her hands found their way to his neck, pulling him closer, closer, and Lawrence gloried in the way she felt.

Oh, he had not kissed a woman in months—but this was no haphazard kiss he would take now and forget about tomorrow.

Forget about Jules? Forget the warmth of her body, the ardor by which she returned his kiss, the passion pouring between them as they stood in the middle of Hyde Park—

And it was that thought which made Lawrence, regretfully, end this madness.

He let go of Julia and half stepped, half staggered back several paces.

Julia's bonnet was crooked, and her eyes were wide as she stared. "Why did you stop?"

Lawrence tried to speak, but at first, he could only breathe a laugh. "Because...damn, Jules, you know full well—"

"I know nothing of the sort," Julia said, a flirtatious air in her voice. "Did—did I not do it right?"

Closing his eyes for a moment in an attempt to get his balance, Lawrence wondered whether any woman had ever kissed so perfectly, so utterly, so innocently. With fire that promised such sweet pleasure if they continued. He would have to try desperately not to think of her tonight.

He opened his eyes and saw shame in her eyes.

"You were perfect," Lawrence said quietly.

The shame disappeared, but she said quietly, "You're just saying that."

"No, I shouldn't be saying that," he admitted darkly, running a hand through his unruly hair.

Blast, this had suddenly got very complicated. Kissing women...well, most of the boxers who earned a little coin spent it on food, beer, and women, and sometimes not always in that order.

But he had stayed away, stayed focused on the task at hand. He was only in this dangerous position because he was attempting to catch an even more dangerous man.

A dangerous situation he was in because he chose to be, eyes wide open, knowing all the facts. Facts Julia did not know.

"This cannot happen again."

The words had slipped from his mouth before he realized he had said them.

Lawrence watched as a dark cloud covered Julia's expression.

"And why not?" she asked boldly.

How had no one married this woman, Lawrence found himself wondering. Beautiful, yes, clearly from a good family, but Miss Julia Dryden was far more than that. Bolder than any woman he had ever known, confident in a way that was highly desirable.

And yet unmarried?

It was difficult not to be impressed, but that did not mean he could entangle her in a web of lies, deceit, and danger that he would certainly not wish his own sister to become involved with.

That was why he had not even told his sister he was here.

"Because," Lawrence said, trying not to notice just how eager his hands were to return to Julia's waist, "you should not be kissing random men."

It sounded foolish, obvious as he said it aloud, but evidently not to the woman standing before him.

Julia arched an eyebrow. "Oh, good. That's easy enough, then."

Despite himself, Lawrence was piqued. Was it truly that easy to forget him? To leave behind such an intense moment of pleasure when he had been certain they had both shared in it?

"I'll just kiss you," said Julia simply, mischief dancing in her eyes. "Shall we return to Rotten Row, or do you wish to kiss a little longer first?"

Lawrence nodded weakly. Perhaps this was the most dangerous part of his life. This woman. This maddening woman.

CHAPTER SIX

February 1, 1810

I T WAS ALMOST midnight when Julia slowly opened the side gate. It creaked. Loudly.

Julia halted, freezing in the cold night air as she looked up at the windows, desperately concerned a light would appear. After all, it had been a loud noise—at least, it had felt like it.

Perhaps she was overthinking. Julia's breath blossomed out before her, the wintery air ice cold as she stood motionless, praying desperately no one had heard her.

If they did, they showed no sign. Slowly, slowly, desperately trying to remind herself she needed to ask a footman to oil the gate in the morning, Julia crept around the side of the house and let herself in through the side door.

It was unlocked. Of course it was. People who lived in their area of London did not worry about locking their doors. Ruffians and the like simply weren't countenanced. Not in Mayfair.

Julia smiled as she slipped off her shoes and crept along the pitch-black corridor.

Ruffians like the people she had just spent the evening with, for example...

Her heart raced as she slowly made her way up the stairs. She was almost safe. If her mother found her here, she could just about explain her presence out of bed by saying she had wanted to go to the kitchen for a drink.

And had…got dressed to do so?

Julia cursed her foolish idea as she reached the landing. She really would have to think of a better excuse, in case she was discovered out of bed. It would be most unfortunate if she was to be found with no snappy retort.

By the time she reached her bedchamber and slowly turned the handle, the exhaustion Julia had kept at bay all evening rushed upon her. She half sat, half fell onto her bed. The hot brick at the end was stone cold.

A smile crept across her face.

And what an evening it had been. Why, she had never seen such complexity of movements as the second fight of the night. Lawrence had said so, too, pointing out the delicate way the man's feet had moved across the ring. He had leaned close to her, pointing, and she had leaned into him. Breathed in the heady sensation of him. Tried to focus on what he was trying to show her when all she could think about was that kiss…

A kiss that, sadly, had never been repeated. *At least, not yet.*

Julia sighed happily.

She had not told Lawrence she was going to be there, and he had not appeared surprised when she had slid onto the bench beside him. It had become their habit, twice a week or so, to meet there. To watch a few fights, talk a little, laugh…and then he would disappear and appear in the ring himself.

Cheering him from the stands was entirely different now she knew him.

Or at least, Julia reminded herself as she slipped off her stockings and started to unpick the ties of her gown, *she knew him better.*

There was still so much she did not know, so much she—

Her bedchamber door opened, and Julia whirled around, pulling her gown around her, but her heart slowed as she saw a familiar grin in the door.

"I heard you come in," whispered Donald with a stifled laugh. "You are incorrigible!"

"And you are the one who took me there first, so it is all your fault," Julia hissed back, trying not to laugh herself.

How fortunate it was that her brother had come of age so recently. To think, if he had not, she would not have been able to go to Almonry Den.

Never met Lawrence…

"You didn't go back again tonight?"

Julia nodded, exhausted. "And I'll be there tomorrow, if you want a flutter."

The terminology tasted strange in her mouth, but it was worth it to see her brother's eyes widen. "Julia Dryden, you cannot possibly—"

"Fine, I won't gamble," sighed Julia. "But you have to admit, it is a wonderful escapade. I enjoy it there."

The laughter slowly ebbed away in her brother's eyes, leaving something that looked to Julia almost like…*severity?*

"You didn't go back to see *him*, did you?"

A prickle of discomfort settled in her chest as Julia dropped her gaze to her hands.

She had, of course. *How could she stay away from Lawrence?* He was the most fascinating man she had ever met. Far more interesting than any gentleman she'd been introduced to, more dangerous, more exciting.

More handsome. More able to make every part of her shiver whenever he sat by her.

And that kiss—

"You mean Lawrence?" she whispered, far more boldly than she felt.

Donald shook his head with a sigh. "You really shouldn't—"

"There are plenty of things a lady should not do, and I would adhere to the rules if I thought a single gentleman would," Julia retorted, trying her best to keep her voice down.

If their mother heard their conversation...

Well. She would not see Lawrence again or attend a single boxing match at the Almonry Den, because she would be restricted to her bedchamber, or worse, buried.

Her brother gazed at her sternly. "As your brother it is my duty—"

"As your older sister, it is my duty to send you to bed," hissed Julia, adopting a mock serious tone as she giggled. "Go on with you, I'm tired. We can discuss this in the morning."

Donald sighed. "Night, Julia."

"Night, Don."

As the door shut, Julia waited to hear her brother's footsteps. As she expected, they did not trail off to the left where his bedchamber could be found...but to the right. To the stairs.

He was going out himself, she thought sleepily as she finished undressing and slipped on her nightgown. *A gaming hell, I'm sure. Hark at him, lecturing me about what was appropriate!*

Only when she settled in bed, the covers mercifully warm thanks to her embroidered blanket—something she had hated making—did Julia permit herself to think once again about the man she craved more than any other.

Lawrence.

It was scandalous, she supposed, that she wanted to see him so often. Even if he had been of her class, a gentleman, it would have been rather irregular to see each other so frequently.

But he was not a gentleman, was he? Julia shivered but not with cold as she curled up and thought of those strong hands. Hands that had undoubtedly fought their way out of a pickle not just in the boxing ring, but in the streets.

Hands that knew precisely what they were doing...

By the time Julia awoke, the sun was up and she was toasty warm under the bedclothes—but she was not there for long.

"Eleven?" she had said yesterday, her voice eager as she looked up into Lawrence's dark eyes.

"You should get home," he had warned her, a teasing lilt in his voice.

She had not heeded him, desperate to make him promise. "Eleven o'clock?"

And Lawrence had hesitated, his gaze roving over her, and Julia had hoped he liked what he saw. He must have done. He had agreed.

They would meet at Hyde Park Corner the next day at eleven o'clock. That was today.

"Darling, I missed you at supper last night," her mother called as Julia raced down the stairs two at a time. "Really, is that the way a lady—"

"Can't stop, Mama, sorry, meeting a—a friend," Julia called out as she rushed into the hall.

Her fingers stumbled as she attempted to pull on her pelisse and pin on her bonnet at the same time. She was going to be late if she did not hurry. *That's what came of going to bed so late...*

"A friend?"

Julia rolled her eyes as she shoved an arm through her pelisse and almost dropped her reticule. "That is what I said, Mama."

Her mother poked her head around the corner of the door to the breakfast room with a most puzzled expression. "But you aren't meeting any friends today, I have a different schedule planned!"

"Well, I am sorry, Mama," Julia said smartly, ramming her bonnet on her head and giving up on the pins.

Her heart pattered excitedly, anticipation mounting. *Just a few more minutes, maybe thirty, and she would see him again...*

"But—"

"Mama, you do not orchestrate my social calendar, I am almost one and twenty," Julia said firmly, turning to look at her mother. "If you wish to include me on invitations, you have to tell me!"

Mrs. Dryden blinked. "But I did. I told you yesterday. We are having elevenses with the Hargreaves and then afternoon tea with the Marnions."

Julia managed to prevent herself from using one of the very colorful curses she had overheard at the Almonry Den. It really was a wonderful sound, she greatly wished to try it out herself, but perhaps a discussion with her mother was not the time.

"I apologize, Mama, but I cannot get out of this now, and you will be more than enough company for the Marnions," she said, stepping toward the door. *Anything to be closer to him...* "And the Hargreaves."

"Julia Dryden," her mother said sternly. "You said that Easter this year was more than enough time to find a husband! I do not wish to choose one for you, but you are getting on in years, dear, and—"

Julia winced. No one wished to be reminded of such a thing. "I will find a husband when I am good and ready, Mama."

"But—"

"I'll see you at dinner!" Julia shot over her shoulder as she slammed the door behind her.

If the door had remained open, she was certain to have heard her mother's outrage—but, as it was, she could ignore her and stride down the street in the bitter cold, toward the person she had not stopped thinking about since the moment she had left him.

"You are late," Lawrence said reprovingly as she rushed toward him, half skipping, half running.

Julia grinned as she tried to catch her breath, leaning a hand against his chest. "Ladies are never late."

"Oh, really?"

There was such laughter in his words Julia hardly knew what to do with herself. What did ladies do, when they met a man who so utterly captivated them? Who proved the rest of the world to be dull?

"Really!" beamed Julia as she looked into the handsome face of a man she was rapidly starting to rely on. "You are early, shamefully so. Your eagerness to be in my presence is noted."

She had meant it as a joke, an encouragement to laugh and tease her some more.

And yet, he didn't. Lawrence flushed, a dark flush across his cheeks, and for some reason it made Julia feel...

Well. As though she was floating.

"Early or late, let's get on," said Lawrence gruffly, and Julia was delighted to see he was still blushing.

He offered his arm. Julia took it, charmed by the way the movement was so natural, so easy.

They walked in silence for a few minutes. Though the day was bright, it was freezing cold. Julia was thankful she had stuffed her gloves into her reticule at some point, for she retrieved them and placed them on.

The only downside, of course, was that she now could not feel the coarseness of Lawrence's coat under her fingertips...or anything more...

"You were not discovered last night?"

Julia shook her head. "No, I do not think so. Well, Donald heard me, but he doesn't count."

Lawrence laughed. "I am not sure, based on my admittedly limited knowledge of your brother, that he would be particularly pleased with being told he doesn't count."

She squeezed his arm in silent reproof. "You know what I mean."

They continued along the path, which was almost empty despite the fashionable hour. *Almost alone*, Julia could not help but think. Not quite as alone as when she had stolen a kiss ...or had he stolen it from her?

She could hardly remember now. Though the moment was in some ways burned into her memory, something she would enjoy over and over again, it was at the same time a rush of sensations she could not untangle.

"Tell me about yourself," Julia said impulsively.

Lawrence raised his eyebrows. "I beg your pardon?"

She smiled at the formal phrase. It was so endearing about the man. He was such an oddity—a medley of well-born and ill-bred, formality and nonsensical informality. He treated her as a lady but was certainly no gentleman.

"I know so little about you," Julia explained as they slowly turned a corner, the path meandering to the right. "We talk of the boxing, of the fighters—"

"Topics you ask me about," Lawrence pointed out.

She shivered as she felt as well as heard his deep voice rumbling through her arm.

"I know that," she said. "It's just...I want to know about that, all of it. But I also want to know about you."

Julia almost held her breath as Lawrence looked at her, eyes serious. Could he see in her face, hear in her voice, just what she wanted?

She hardly knew herself. All she could fathom was that spending time with Lawrence was fast becoming the only thing she wanted to do with her days.

Something her mother would certainly not approve of...

Lawrence shrugged. "There's not much to tell."

"There must be something," Julia persisted. Just why she was pushing this, she could hardly tell, but she craved to know more. To know everything about the tall, dark man beside her.

He laughed. "I am not so interesting as you may think."

"But you have a past."

The arm she was holding stiffened. "What makes you say that?"

Julia bit her lip. *She had not intended it to sound like...well, what it sounded like.*

Besides, she was not accusing him of anything. In truth, it was rather exciting to think that the man with whom she was walking had a murky and rather dangerous beginning.

It excited something in her that had been awoken the moment she had first seen Lawrence in the boxing ring.

"I just meant you have parents, perhaps siblings," Julia said, trying to keep her voice calm. "You didn't grow up in London or else you would have the accent of the East End."

Lawrence snorted. "No! No, I didn't grow up here."

An icy wind blew, and Julia stepped closer to him, instinctively eager for his warmth. He did not move away, and her heart skipped a beat as she felt the intimacy of what she had done.

What he had allowed her to do.

"So?" she persisted. "Where did you grow up?"

Julia glanced up as she spoke, trying to ascertain from his face whether he was amused by her questions, offended, or something in between.

But there was a shadow on his face, a darkness she had not expected. Wherever it had been, it had not been happy.

"A long way from here," Lawrence said quietly. "In the north."

"The north?" Julia repeated. That was certainly not what she had expected. There was no northern twang in the man's accent, nothing in his way of speaking that spoke of a northern clime. "Truly?"

A wry smile creased Lawrence's lips. "Truly. And that's all you need to know."

"But—"

"I don't talk about myself much, Julia," he said quietly.

Julia's shiver had nothing to do with the freezing day. *Would she ever grow accustomed to hearing her name on his lips?*

"I liked it better when you called me Jules," she said shamelessly.

Lawrence squeezed her hand on his arm. "Really."

She swallowed. *Was she going too far?*

"Really," she breathed, then clearing her throat, continued in a firmer voice. "Look, you can't just say that you grew up in the north and leave it at that."

"Why not?"

"Because—because," Julia stammered, absolutely at a loss to explain why.

Because I want to know all about you, she thought wildly. *Because you are the most interesting man I have ever met, yet you defy me at every turn, but you are here, aren't you? With me? You could have made excuses, refused to agree to be here, not turned up…*

And yet you are here.

Lawrence grinned. "I usually let me hands do the talking."

Julia rolled her eyes. "That's just what a man of your class would say."

Only when the words had slipped from her lips did she hear them.

"That's just what a man of your class would say."

Lawrence made no movement, save a small eyebrow raise. He did not remove her hand from his arm. He said nothing, did not berate her for the way she had spoken, chastise her for such rudeness.

In a way, Julia wished he would. Anything to end the silence, to show how abominably rudely she had spoken.

To make it easier for her to apologize, admit she had been wrong.

She had never been particularly good at apologizing. Saying sorry was something she had been forced to do as a child, even when not in the wrong, and it had irritated her to no end.

But in this case, she was quite firmly in the wrong.

Julia took a deep breath. "I-I am sorry."

Lawrence was quiet for a moment. "It must take a great deal for a woman of your standing to say that. To a man like me."

She saw nobility there even if his upbringing did not bestow it. When had she ever looked so closely at a man who was not a gentleman?

Perhaps she never had.

Because Lawrence was…noble. Far nobler than the pawing gentlemen at Almack's, or those who attempted to impress her at the card table, or with gossip she would rather not hear.

The wind blew fiercely, rustling Lawrence's dark locks, and Julia felt a desperate need to wend her hands through them once more.

"Tell me," she said quietly. "I want to know."

"Everything?"

Julia smiled nervously. "Anything."

Lawrence sighed heavily and shook his head with a rueful smile. "You simply don't give up, do you?"

"Not when I know what I want," she said quietly.

His gaze met hers, and for a moment Julia was certain she was going to rise in the air, all gravity forgotten, just at the way he looked at her.

"I grew up...in the north," said Lawrence quietly. "Come on, let's sit here."

Hyde Park was almost empty; it was not difficult to find an empty bench. Julia tried her best to sit as close to Lawrence as possible, while still retaining some societal dignity if someone was to see them.

Or, God forbid, Lady Romeril.

"The north," she prompted.

Lawrence grinned as he leaned back. "Have you ever been?"

Julia shook her head. "All I've ever known is London. I went to Brighton once a few years ago, but only for a week."

"Well, the north is nothing like Brighton," said Lawrence, his grin deepening. "It's far wilder and more beautiful, in my opinion. Moors that run into the horizon as far as the eye can see, sweet-smelling heather, and crispy gorse that will catch at your clothes, trying to keep you there."

He glanced at Julia, as though afraid he had already said too much. Julia nodded encouragingly, enchanted by his words.

"The land there is far wilder than anything in the south," Lawrence continued, his shoulders loosening as he relaxed.

Julia watched, hardly able to take her eyes from him.

"And beaches—"

"Beaches? In the north?"

His laughter made heat sear Julia's cheeks. "You think we don't have coastline up there?"

Julia glanced at her hands, ashamed at her ignorance. "Of course, I—go on."

"Well, the beaches there are northern, so they are different. Stronger currents, deeper tides." Lawrence smiled, almost wistfully. "And the forests, absolutely packed with animals, waterfalls, majestic mountains which rise out of the mist. Once, when I was hunting—"

"Hunting?"

Julia had not been able to help interrupting, but her curiosity was so great. *Hunting? A man like Lawrence?*

And all the tension crept back into their conversation. Lawrence's smile was gone, a look of almost astonishment in his eyes.

"I did not mean hunting," he said hurriedly.

Julia frowned. "Then what did you—"

"I mean, when the local lords went hunting, and I-I beat the bushes to make the grouse fly up," said Lawrence quickly.

Too quickly.

Julia swallowed. It was none of her business, his past, not truly. But it was not difficult to put two and two together.

"But you have a past."

"What makes you say that?"

"Once, when I was hunting—"

Yes, he had been hunting, but not on his own land. Poaching was a terrible crime, punishable by imprisonment, as far as she knew.

No wonder he had flushed at the accidental slip. No wonder he had been forced away from the land he so evidently loved, to come down to London where anonymity would protect him.

Julia smiled. "Tell me about these moors."

Lawrence met her eyes, and she tried her best to show him she held no danger for him. Why, quite to the contrary. She was far more likely to be in danger from him.

A slow smile crept across his face. "When you go out on the moors in summer..."

CHAPTER SEVEN

February 3, 1810

L AWRENCE STARED AT the note delivered by an unnamed rascal who had slipped into the wilderness of the street before he'd had time to take in more than a scrap of dark hair and filthy hands.

There were dirty fingerprints all over the paper, but the writing was still legible, even if the letter itself was rather blunt.

Lawrence.

He is in London. I received word from a boat that brought him across, and there is nowhere else we would expect him to be. Why have you not found him? Why is he not yet brought to justice?

Focus on the job at hand and do not permit anything to distract you. It would be death to another, surely, if you are unable to apprehend him.

Do not forget what he has done.

Dulverton

Lawrence read the note three more times to commit it to memory, then scrunched it up and threw it into the meager fire he had managed to build in the fireplace. A more impressive blaze scalded through his veins, anger overwhelming him.

Well, what in God's name did they think he was doing? Just living here in squalor for the fun of it? Abandoning his name and luxurious life simply because he had nothing better to do?

Leaving his sister in her grief as they both mourned their murdered brother?

Lawrence's jaw tightened as he leaned back heavily in his armchair. *Well. Perhaps there was a small element of truth in that last one.*

It had been painful, being home, watching his sister fall apart after the loss of their elder brother. Seeing her mourn as he could not bring himself to mourn. Seeing her grieve when it had felt, in some way he could not explain, that it was his fault.

Pain. His fingers hurt. Lawrence looked down to see he had been gripping his fists so tightly, his nails had dug into his palms.

Slowly, he managed to uncurl his fingers and saw half-moons of beading blood.

Damn. That was going to hurt the next time he stepped into the ring, which would be...

A quick glance at his pocket watch drew a groan from his lips. He was supposed to be in the ring in fifteen minutes. A good thing Alan had insisted on him taking lodgings so close to the damned place. A few streets away, and he may not have managed it.

After ducking past two carriages, avoiding a scrapping fight over the price of beef, and dodging a pickpocket who was about to relieve a gentleman of his wallet—a gentleman dressed much as Lawrence would have been...

The Duke of Penshaw stepped into Almonry Den.

Lawrence breathed it in. Strange, that after six months this place had become home in much the same way the Dulverton Club or Penshaw Place.

He knew the smell of the straw, the sawdust, the sweat of the men in the ring, the excitement of the crowd. The particularly sour ale that was served by grinning women with dirt-flecked shawls, the sharp notes of pastry as pies were passed along rows, thruppenny bits thrown down in recompense.

This was starting to become all he knew.

And it would stay that way, Lawrence told himself firmly as he strode over to the ring, pushing his way past the crowd as he got closer, *until he found Mortimer.*

He had to be here somewhere. If Dulverton was sure he was in England, he was in London. There was nowhere else for the damned blaggard to go.

And here was the only place Mortimer had friends—at least, acquaintances which could almost be guaranteed not to reveal his presence to the authorities.

"There you are!" Alan's relief was palpable, the back of his hand wiping sweat from his brow. "I was almost about to enter the ring on your behalf!"

Lawrence snorted as he patted his boxing coach on the back. "Never fear, I wouldn't let them eat you."

The older man raised an eyebrow. "You think I wouldn't survive in there?"

Instead of replying, Lawrence glanced up at the ring in which at that very moment two men were pummeling each other viciously. A tooth flew up in the air in a terrible arc as the crowd jeered.

He looked back at Alan, who had the good grace to shrug. "Fair point. You ready?"

Lawrence nodded. "Of course."

It was a lie, one he had become accustomed to telling in the last few weeks.

Ready? Ready to fight, yes, ready to try and keep an eye out for the damned man he was seeking. Ready to exchange muttered words of congratulation or commiseration to the other boxers, to befriend them, to hear if they had heard anything...

But in the last fortnight, things had changed, and Lawrence was not about to admit it.

Because he was here for another reason, wasn't he?

Julia Dryden.

Lawrence tried to swallow, but his mouth had gone dry at the very thought of her name. *Her name? Dear God, he was losing all touch with reality if her mere name could overpower him.* He was supposed to be a renowned boxer.

"Shall we return to Rotten Row, or do you wish to kiss a little longer first?"

He shivered. He groaned slightly, the noise hidden by the shouting masses, and despite himself, Lawrence's gaze drifted toward the crowd.

Was she there? Was it possible he would be watched by her, as he so dearly wished to observe her?

"Ready?"

"Wh-What?" Lawrence said, turning round hastily.

Alan was frowning again. "You've got awful jumpy these last few days, boy. Are you sure you aren't having…second thoughts?"

The memory of the note he had received not twenty minutes ago rang through Lawrence's mind.

Focus on the job at hand and do not permit anything to distract you. It would be death to another, surely, if you are unable to apprehend him.

Do not forget what he has done.

He was not here to become distracted by a woman. He was not here to be dazzled by a pretty face, or a pretty nature—or a woman who felt delectable under his—

Lawrence swallowed. He was here to find a murderer, a traitor to the British Crown.

Not take a romp with a lady who had no idea he was a duke.

"I'm ready," he said, far more firmly than he felt.

Alan hesitated, then glanced up at the ring as the victor proudly promenaded out… and the loser was dragged along the floor. "If your head is not—"

"I'm fine, Alan, trust me," Lawrence said, allowing just a little of the haughtiness he had been known for when living under his true name to seep through.

He pulled a hand through his wild hair and hoped to goodness no one could sense the wild butterflies rushing in his stomach. Nothing to do with the impending fight and everything to do with the hopes of seeing a pretty young woman.

Thankfully, it appeared his boxing coach was satisfied.

"Go on then," barked Alan. "And give him what for!"

Lawrence heard the rising cry of excitement from the crowd as he stepped under the rope and into the ring, and though he knew he was only here to enact justice on an evil man, he could not help his stomach turning with pride of his own.

They adored him, revered him—betted against him, often, but Lawrence did not mind.

At least here he could leave behind his worries, his mind's constant whirling, his obsession with vengeance and easily distractable loins, and focus on two things.

Spotting Mortimer in the crowd.

And punching the man before him as hard as he could.

It was therefore quite unfortunate that as his fresh opponent, a man he suspected was called Tom but could not be certain, had stepped into the ring, Lawrence's eye had been caught by a figure in the crowd.

And not a tall dark man with a scar just above his eye.

"Go on, Lawrence!" cried Julia with a wide grin, her hands clapping along with those of the rest of the spectators. *So how could he hear hers clearly above all the rest?* "Come on, Lawrence!"

Lawrence stumbled as he stepped forward to shake the man's hand. Jeers mingled with the cheers.

"Drank too much already?" sneered Tom, grasping his hand and squeezing it so tightly, Lawrence was amazed his fingers were still attached.

He did not deign to reply, merely squeezed back equally as hard, then released the man before turning to wait for the bell.

"Ohh!"

The crowd gasped as Tom did not bother for such niceties. A heavy fist pummeled the back of Lawrence's head, causing stars to appear, and he stumbled, trying to find his footing as Alan shouted something, but he could not make out the words and—

Wham! Lawrence coughed as his stomach rippled with the pain of the punch he had just taken to his side, but he had managed to find his footing now, twisting around to face his foe.

Tom was grinning. "What are you, some sort of gentleman who waits for a bell?"

Lawrence did not bother pointing out that regardless of the fact that he was, actually, a gentleman, there were bets being taken on this match and it behooved them to play fairly. There was no point. One did not engage in reasonable discourse with men like Tom.

Squaring himself up, lifting up his hands to his face in preparation for a punch Lawrence was sure would knock the man to the ground, it was indeed unfortunate that just above Tom's shoulder was...

His stomach lurched. *Julia.* She was standing now, her blue gown a shimmering refuge of color in the dark, her eyes wide with fear for him, her lips—

The next punch rocked his head so severely that he fell.

Lawrence breathed in sawdust, heard celebration far off as his head spun, and it was only a few minutes later that he had sufficient wherewithal to rise.

Alan was shaking his head. "You lost focus there, my boy, and—"

"Lawrence! Lawrence, are you quite well?"

Lawrence smiled bitterly as he sat on the edge of the ring, slipping down to stand beside his boxing coach and a beautiful woman who had rushed over, it seemed, the moment he had taken a tumble.

Well, damn. It was bad enough that Julia—that *Miss Dryden*, he had to at least attempt some sort of decorum—had seem him knocked down once. Did she really have to see it again?

It wasn't just his jaw that was smarting. It was his pride.

"You are quite well, aren't you?" Julia said anxiously.

Lawrence tried to remind himself that he was supposed to be hunting a murderer. His brother's murderer.

If only Julia did not smell so wonderfully of…was that lavender?

"I said," Alan said, a little testily now as the crowd roared around them, another fight about to commence, "you lost focus there. I wonder why."

His gaze fell heavily on the woman between them.

Lawrence smiled weakly. *Well, what was he supposed to say? How could he deny it?*

"I am quite well," he said to Julia, ignoring the throbbing pain in his side and the sense he had bitten his own tongue.

"Come, you need fresh air, you cannot possibly stay here," she said, slipping her hand into his.

Lawrence stared down at their hands, his hand and hers. Entangled so naturally, so easily, it was like breathing. No one had ever taken his hand before.

"Madgwick, I really—"

"I'll see you later, Alan," Lawrence found himself saying as he was led carefully by the hand that felt so warm in his. "Tomorrow."

"But Lawrence—"

"I really shouldn't go with you," murmured Lawrence to the woman who so expertly weaved her way through the crowd, Alan's words disappearing behind them.

It was outrageous, really. He had a job to do. There was no point in being here, undercover, if he was going to permit himself to wander off in the middle of bouts.

Yet how could he deny what was happening right now?

Oh, not the fact that he was leaving with Julia. As they stepped out onto the street, the fresh air filled his lungs. But that wasn't what he was most conscious of. No, it was the way his heart was beating rapidly, how irregular it had become. No amount of fighting, of twists and turns in the ring, created this sense of heady giddiness, of joy, of almost…euphoria.

Julia grinned. "You may thank me for rescuing you later."

"I think I'll thank you now," Lawrence said honestly, breathing in the admittedly less fresh air than he had supposed. A horse had recently done its business just a few feet away. "But I cannot permit you to—"

"I did not ask your permission, so you do not need to give it," Julia said quietly, her smile softening, but if anything, becoming more mischievous. "Come on."

It did not occur to Lawrence to inquire where they were going. It did not appear, in fact, that Julia knew. At least, he could not imagine she frequented these streets often, not with her breeding.

And so they meandered. Only after about a minute did Lawrence realize, with some sadness, that Julia had released her hand from his grip. The fact she had immediately slipped it into his arm was small comfort.

"That's a bit better. Somewhere you can walk it off. Now, Lawrence, tell me," said Julia finally, as they promenaded along a street that was a little more reputable. "How do you make a living?"

He had to laugh. "Does it ever occur to you that you ask the most inappropriate questions?"

She looked up into his eyes, and Lawrence's stomach lurched as his gaze met hers. A twist in his soul, a heartbeat skipped over, and he looked away.

He was not falling in—no. That was nonsense. He had more important things to be doing that finding young ladies attractive!

If only he could persuade his mind not to notice the gentle swell of her breasts, the curve of her cheek as she laughed, the way she had pressed her lips against his own…

"Yes, I am rather forward," Julia said with a dry laugh. "My mother, she…she always…"

And just like that, the light within her went out.

Lawrence almost stumbled, his attention was so wholly focused on the woman beside him rather than where his feet should be going.

It was astounding. Never before had he seen such an immediate change. All at once, the glow of excitement within her disappeared, the joy she had been radiating was gone.

Now a woman who was but a shell of the Julia he was getting to know walked beside him, head lowered, eyes downcast.

Lawrence swallowed. He had never…well. He had bedded many a woman, but actually courting?

Not that this was—oh hell's bells.

How was he supposed to ask what had clouded her heart, when she thought him naught but a man who fought for a living?

"I-I win a percentage of the gambling takings," he said quietly. "And I'm paid for each fight. A penny for a loss. A shilling for a win."

Julia looked up, her eyes bright with unshed tears that Lawrence could not understand. *What had her mother said?*

"And is that enough?"

Lawrence laughed dryly. *Enough?* Dear God, he spent more in candles in a month at Penshaw Place than he was earning a week at the moment.

Thank goodness Alan had taught him a few ways to make the pennies go further.

"I survive," he said cagily. His curiosity prodded him to ask, "You were about to say something about your mother, just then."

And there it was again. There had been a brief spark of interest as he had explained his—temporary—income, but the moment he mentioned her mother, it was gone.

Julia shook her head as she looked away at the pavement on the other side of the street. "It's nothing."

Lawrence bit down the instinct to immediately say it was certainly not nothing, and that he wanted to hear all about it. All about her. Know her dreams and hopes and pressures. Understand what she loved and what she reviled. Hear the whispers of her heart.

Because there was surely something deeper here, something about her that—

"Mothers," said Julia darkly, "always have plans, don't they?"

Her eyes blazed with a sort of anger Lawrence had never seen before. His breath caught in his throat, his entire being attuned to her frustration, though what she could possibly be frustrated about he could not tell.

After all, she was a well-dressed, well-spoken lady. She evidently had much independence, or else she would never have made her way to the Almonry Den in the first place.

Her brother was a little...lax, Lawrence thought ruefully. But then who was he to judge? He had left his own sister for six months, and she had little idea where he was.

"I don't really know," he said honestly, for it was quite clear by the look on Julia's face that she was expecting a reply. "My mother died when she gave birth to my sister, I was only a few years old."

The anger in Julia's face softened. "I am sorry."

He shrugged. "I used to think one could not miss what one did not know, but now I am not so sure. Plenty of men have mothers—I mean, everyone does, obviously—but many of us are raised without mothers. If yours is...overbearing..."

It had been a guess, that was all, but Lawrence was almost certain he was correct—and Julia's dry laugh seemed to confirm it.

"Overbearing is not quite the right word," she said dryly as they stepped around a corner, their pace slowing as their conversation continued. "I mean, yes, mothers surely have a right to dictate some of their children's lives—not that I suppose you would know much about that. You chart your own course, choose your own destiny."

Julia's voice was almost wistful, but Lawrence stiffened. *What had she guessed?* Had he been too polite, too formal? Had there been a mannerism as yet undetected that had betrayed him?

"What do you mean?"

She smiled softly. "Why, just that you are a man. Men do not get told what to do, where to go, who to—but hark at me, wittering on. You don't want to hear that."

Lawrence acted instinctively. "Yes, I do."

He had halted, and thanks to his grip on her arm, had halted her, too. Julia stared, almost nervously, but that was his own fault. His gaze darted down to her lips, and a hint of longing must have shown on his face.

He wanted her. God knew how he should not even be touching her now, how he should be back in that ring fighting for his life and looking for a killer.

But here, with Julia…

"And what would you be doing, if you were not fighting? As a boxer, I mean?"

Lawrence swallowed. Ah. Now that was an interesting question. "Do?"

Julia nodded. "Everyone has to earn a living—at least, if not a gentleman."

This was the trouble with a cover story like his, Lawrence thought darkly. He and Alan had not considered much beyond the fact that he had left the north needing work, and had found it at the Almonry Den.

He had not expected conversations to reach any sort of depth that would require more.

"Lawrence?"

"I—I suppose I would be working," Lawrence invented wildly, trying not to think of the truth. Dancing at Almack's, gambling at the Old Duke's, trying not to get caught in a mama's scheme to marry…

"Working. Yes."

The trouble was, Julia was not that foolish. She smiled. "You're hiding something."

Lawrence stiffened. "So are you."

The answer came to his lips without conscious thought, but the arrow evidently hit home.

Julia laughed, then turned and started walking, her arm still slipped in his. "Who isn't?"

CHAPTER EIGHT

February 9, 1810

"—AND, OF COURSE, you will then attend tea with Miss Hollingford and her mother, a very fine woman, and I hope you will ensure to mention that, Julia, for it is imperative that she has a positive impression of—Julia, are you attending?"

Julia sighed, plastered a smile on her face, and tried to speak without sarcasm. "How could I not attend, Mama?"

Her mother glared for a moment, then smiled sweetly. "Wonderful. And then after the tea, there is an evening dinner I think will be most suitable, we have been invited to two, but I believe there will be more eligible gentlemen at…"

It was easy to allow the words to wash over her. Julia had heard it all before, anyway. The countless invitations, the dinners, dancing, balls, card parties, walks in Hyde Park, rides—as long as a chaperone could be found, naturally—all designed to elicit one thing.

A proposal of marriage.

Julia shifted uncomfortably on the sofa in the morning room as her mother continued.

"—light cerise gown if you would not mind, I know you prefer the blue, but I truly think your eyes will be highlighted a little better. I know you do not think of these things, but that is what a mother is for,

Julia—Julia, are you still—"

"Yes, Mama, I am listening," Julia interrupted, biting back her frustration and trying to smile. "I am always listening."

Always listening. Well, that was at least true. Always hearing about how her mother's friends' daughters were getting married, or having a third child, or had been whisked off her feet by a duke.

A duke! Julia almost snorted at the very thought. Try as her mother might, they were not the sort to entangle themselves with a duke. They were respectable, yes, gentry, certainly. But dukes?

"—how is the younger Mr. Renwick, do you know?"

Julia blinked. Her mother, her dark brown hair growing silver with each passing month but her eyes just as fierce, just as determined, was examining her with a raised eyebrow.

"I beg your pardon?" Julia was forced to ask weakly.

Mrs. Dryden glowered. "I knew it! I knew you were not listening—Donald, did I not say—"

"Oh, what a shame, Mama, I find I am needed elsewhere," said Donald, hastily rising and abandoning his newspaper with as much disdain with which he now abandoned Julia.

She rose, too. "I shall accompany you, Don—"

"You will do no such thing," said their mother sternly, fixing her daughter with a look that forced Julia to fold back onto the sofa. "I have much to say to you, Julia, on the subject of your marriage."

Donald threw her a grin as he slipped out the door, preventing Julia from scowling.

"And there is no need to look so horrifically unhappy about it," smarted Mrs. Dryden. "Ladies your age *want* to get married!"

Julia swallowed. It was not a topic she wished to discuss—at least, not with her mother. Though the topic had been overwhelming her every movement for the last year and a half, it had a strange sort of resonance now.

Now that she had met...

"You're hiding something."

"So are you."

"Who isn't?"

Julia cleared her throat and swiftly picked up a book to hide behind.

Not that it would do much good. It was not just her mother's ire she was attempting to escape but her own thoughts, and they crowded her mind as swiftly as her heartbeat raced.

Lawrence Madgwick. He was a rather unfortunate complication.

She had never considered herself romantic. Never thought dreamily of a prince sweeping her away from it all, or a tall handsome duke promising her the world.

Why, she would not have the faintest idea what to say to a duke!

But Julia was no fool. Though dukes and princes were out of the question, someone like Lawrence was equally out of bounds.

A man like that, who worked with his hands—worse, who fought for a living!

Yet something drew her to him. Something she should fight, she knew, but she could not. Julia had never been forced to decide between what she wanted, and...

Her gaze fell on her mother, who looked up as Julia rose from the sofa.

"Where are you going?"

"To Mr. Rivers, the haberdasher," Julia lied, tasting the bitterness of the untruth on her tongue.

She hated to do it. She was unaccustomed to falsehood of any kind, but she could hardly speak truthfully about her intended destination.

Her mother's face visibly relaxed. "Ah, that is quite understandable. Seeking a few ribbons for tonight's adventure?"

Julia nodded, not revealing she had already entirely forgotten what that evening's adventure was supposed to be. If she were fortunate, she could "forget" to return home...

"Well, add it to the Dryden tab, and I shall ensure to close it at the end of the month," said Mrs. Dryden generously. "If that is what is needed to find you a husband, then it is money well spent. Go on then, dear. And take an umbrella, it is sure to rain."

Just a hint of guilt seared Julia's heart as she pulled on her pelisse and slipped an umbrella over her arm.

Lying to her mother...it felt wrong. It was wrong.

Yet not seeing Lawrence for so many days was so much more wrong. She yearned for him, needed to be close to him, needed to hear his voice.

Feel his touch...

By the time she had reached the Almonry Den, her feet taking her far swifter now she was accustomed to the way, Julia had promised herself two things.

Firstly, this would be the last time she would actively seek out Lawrence Madgwick. It was madness, purposefully hoping to spend time with a man! Not even a gentleman, though there was something in him that suggested good breeding, even if all the evidence pointed to the contrary.

And secondly, she would finally this evening have a heart-to-heart conversation with her mother, and tell her once and for all that if she married, it would be to a gentleman of her own choosing, in her own time.

Both of these promises fell to the wayside as Julia stepped inside, breathed in the sawdust, and saw...Lawrence.

Julia gasped. It was a side of Lawrence she had never seen before. The place was almost empty; it was too early for any fights. There was no crowd seated on the benches, no roaring, no jeering, no hasty bets being taken as fists flew through the air.

In fact, there was almost no one there at all.

Which was why, perhaps, Lawrence had considered this the perfect time to practice.

Julia slipped soundlessly onto a bench in a dark corner, eyes fixed on him. His breeches tight, his shirt missing, sweat glistening on the muscles that she had felt when they had lost their heads and kissed in Hyde Park.

Her fingers ached to touch them. To feel their strength, their mastery.

Lawrence was moving forward, his feet swift as his hands worked furiously, punching the air. When he reached a certain point, he turned around and punched his way back along the line.

Julia tried to catch her breath, but it was impossible. The physicality of the man, the strength, the power, but also the control, the restraint. He was not punching with his full strength. She could see that in the way his shoulders tensed as he pulled back the punches.

Something ached in her that had never ached before.

If only the place was completely empty.

Now she came to look again, there was only a pair of men chatting away on the other side of the ring. They were paying Lawrence no heed.

If only they would leave. Then, Julia found herself thinking most wantonly...then she could approach Lawrence. Speak to him. Touch him. Kiss him...

"Jules?"

Julia started, almost slipping off the bench. "What?"

As she looked up, she saw Lawrence had spotted her and was laughing at her astonished expression.

"Dear me, what do you think you're doing here?" he said easily, stepping toward her with the self-assurance of a man several times his better, his body glistening with power and temptation. "This is not the place for a lady."

Julia rose to her feet so swiftly, the earth seemed to shift underneath her. *Oh, he had absolutely no idea how little she wanted to be a lady in this moment...*

She was an innocent, yes, but she was no fool. She knew what ladies and gentlemen... but no, that was not quite right.

She knew what men and women, and sometimes women and women, and she had once heard men and men could do with each other. Share with each other. What delight they could give each other.

Julia shivered as Lawrence came to a stop only a few feet away. An arm's length. If she reached out, she could—

"Watching, of course. You never know," she found herself saying, astonished her voice managed to stay so calm. "I might want to fight one day."

Her statement was ridiculous. *Her, fight?* Julia could not think of a single situation in which that would be necessary. Besides the fact that ladies simply did not get involved in such nonsense, she had her brother. Donald would fight for her, if ever a fight was needed.

But what, a small voice in her mind whispered, *if you were not with Donald?* What if you were with Lawrence? His arm around you while his other hand fought off attackers, and as they lay at your feet, he would kiss her hard on the—

"I pray you never have to fight," Lawrence said easily, tilting his head slightly as he examined her. "That cannot be the reason you were watching me."

Julia cursed the fact that she had allowed her curiosity—no, *her desire, at least in the privacy of her own mind she could be honest*—to overwhelm her. She did not need Lawrence knowing just how much she wanted to watch him! To look at him. To see all of him...

Flushing furiously as her gaze dropped, almost against her will, to the front of his breeches, Julia forced herself to look away—and saw something perhaps just as interesting.

The pair of men who had been discussing something by the ring were leaving. In about five seconds, she and Lawrence would be completely alone.

And he was still not wearing a shirt.

"I suppose I should learn to fight."

Lawrence snorted. "Jules, you'll...well. You have your brother to fight for you, and one day, you'll have…"

A husband. The words were not spoken, but they hung in the air as clear as day, making Julia's cheeks darken.

"I suppose so," she said quietly.

"You don't want a husband?"

How could he ask her such a question? It took all Julia's self-control to speak calmly, rather than rage against his presumption. His presumption that she had not thought of him in such a way…

"Yes," she admitted quietly. "I…well, I always thought I would get married. I hoped, despite my station in life, for a love match."

Her eyes cautiously met his, and she was astonished to find him looking at her closely.

"Love matches aren't for the likes of you," he said quietly.

A shiver rushed up her spine. "What do you mean?"

"Ladies and gentlemen," Lawrence said in a low voice. "There's little choice, from what I see. A gilded cage, no opportunity to fight for what you want."

Her heart soared. "But you can. Fight for what you want, I mean. Who you want."

Try as she might, she could not keep her voice level. Did he understand? Could he see in her heart was she was trying to—

"So you want to learn to fight?" Lawrence said, changing the subject.

Julia swallowed. He was right. Matrimony was a dangerous subject for anyone, let alone two people from vastly different backgrounds who had most injudiciously kissed. "Of course, it is unlikely I shall ever have to fight, but… you never know. If you truly cared about me, you would teach me."

Her eyes met his, as boldly as she dared, as her lungs tightened with every breath. How could she have said such a thing! How was he supposed to react to her immodest—

"Oh, Julia," murmured Lawrence, almost closing the gap between them. "I care about you more than you know. Probably…no, almost definitely too much."

Julia gasped, fighting for breath as his serious eyes met hers.

Oh, it was too much—and at the same time, not enough. How could she stand it? How was it possible that she was still able to stand as Lawrence stared deeply into her face, his taut stomach muscles twisting as though he fought something just as she did.

Was she imagining it? Was it all in her mind…or was there something stirring a little lower than his stomach?

"God, I shouldn't have said that," Lawrence breathed.

Julia's cheeks were surely red, for they were scalding. "I am glad you did."

"Still," said Lawrence in an undertone. "You are a lady, and I—"

"You are a fighter," she interrupted, her very breath stolen. "Teach me."

He would never do such a thing, and she was foolish to request it. She should not have come here.

Yet as Julia kept Lawrence's gaze, she saw something far more than the base animal instincts. Something…far more noble. Something deeper, darker, and yet more gallant.

Lawrence grinned and held out a hand. "Come on then."

Julia almost stumbled—a habit, it appeared, whenever in Lawrence's presence—as he led her to the open ground where he had been practicing. His hand branded her. When he released it, Julia half expected to see his name seared into her palm.

"Now, you stand like this," Lawrence said in a businesslike manner that roused Julia from her reverie. *Mostly.* "See? Feet like this? More apart."

Julia tried desperately to concentrate, but it was rather difficult when one couldn't see one's feet and a handsome man without a shirt was two feet away from you.

"Yes," she said, hoping to goodness he did not ask her to lift her skirts to show him.

She might just die. Or fall into his arms. Either seemed inappropriate.

"Right, then you'll need to raise your hands up like—no, not like that," Lawrence said with a laugh. "Here."

And before Julia could do anything, before she could explain just how outrageous it was that they were doing this, before she could remind him anyone could come in at any moment, Lawrence had stepped before her and taken her hands in his.

A jolt rushed through her body, and Julia swayed, holding onto Lawrence as though he was the only one who could sustain her. Perhaps he was. His eyes met hers as an aching longing overwhelmed her, and she knew what she needed. She needed him.

"Lawrence," Julia breathed.

She watched him swallow, hoped beyond hope he felt the same. That he could feel the need to be close—was that desire in his eyes? Was she fooling herself, tricking herself into believing what she wanted, rather than what was true?

"Th-Then you need to bunch your f-fingers into fists," Lawrence murmured, his breath as jagged as Julia's felt.

He curled his hands, turning her fingers into fists as his own fingers enclosed hers.

Julia tried to think, she really did, but it was feeling now that was taking over, not thought. Emotion, not reason.

What need had she for reason, when Lawrence was but inches away, his strong chest just waiting to press into hers—

"And then?" Julia whispered. "What do we do next?"

His dark eyes flashed for a moment, but he said not a word. How could he? Julia knew he was suffering, too, his heart surely beating as frantically as her own.

Surely she could not be alone in feeling this way? As though the whole world was now turning not on an axis, but on this point, right here?

"What we do next is...is up to you," Lawrence whispered.

Julia whimpered slightly, unable to keep the need from her throat. How could he do this? Tease her with such closeness, such heady masculinity, then force her to take the next step?

If only he did not look so... If only his scent did not overwhelm her mind, a heady mix of sweat and power, something that overawed her so entirely all reason disappeared.

"I...I..." Julia managed.

Then it was over. The moment was gone, Lawrence was gone, his touch on her hands absent, and she could have cried out with despair. How could he leave her when—

"Let me show you," murmured a voice by her ear.

Julia's eyelashes fluttered shut as Lawrence's strong arms came around her, her pelisse crushed against her as his chest encircled her shoulders.

Oh, this was heavenly. This was certainly not something she had ever felt when discussing art with gentlemen at dinner or trying to laugh at their awful jokes around an afternoon tea.

No other man had ever made her heart sing, her whole body tighten with something that was not pain but appeared to be close...

"Like this," Lawrence said quietly, his breath warming her neck.

Before Julia could point out the impropriety of such a situation— words she had heard her mother use countless times—Lawrence punched forward with his right arm, the gentle force of it encouraging her own right arm to follow suit.

Oh, it was poetry in motion, moving in time with him. A spark of joy rushed through Julia's heart, and she laughed almost with glee at the sense of satisfaction she felt by punching into the air.

"Like that?"

"Just like that," Lawrence said approvingly, his voice soft. "Now your left—"

They both punched forward, Julia overjoyed in the sense of him around her, embracing her, his breath caressing her cheek, his very body acting as a shield against the world.

"And now we step forward."

Julia did not need further explanation, not with the warm yet solid pressure of Lawrence's left leg against hers, pushing her forward.

They moved together, each step punctuated with a punch from the other side, and Julia could almost fly, it was so splendid.

How had she never known this before? The ecstasy of moving in time with another, of seeing their body shift with yours, the sense that in a way, they were one—

"Lawrence," Julia breathed, halting and twisting in his arms to turn to him, to affix her mouth where it needed to be, on his own, needing to taste him, to finally permit herself the relief of kissing him.

He did not move away. His hands met now behind her waist, on her back, encircling her completely. Julia looked up into his face and knew he felt as she did, that something bigger than them, more powerful than them, was drawing them together. It would be foolish to fight it, for who wished to fight fate? One could not punch away providence.

His breathing was quick, his bare chest moving against hers in a delightfully pleasing way. Julia could not understand why the brushing of her breasts against him elicited such a powerful response, but it did, and it would soon overwhelm her.

She needed him to—

"Julia," he said quietly, and he raised a hand to her cheek, cupping it slightly as he dipped his head to—

"Oh, Lawrence—"

"Lawrence! There you are!"

Julia had never known a man to move so quickly. Retreating so rapidly she almost fell, the loss of his secure support gone, Lawrence grinned at the older man she had seen him with so many times.

"Alan! I was just looking for you, Miss Dryden here—"

"Miss Dryden is leaving," snapped the older man, and Julia wilted in the fierce judgment of his gaze. "And Miss Dryden might want to think twice about risking her reputation by being here."

Julia bristled. "I do not think," she began icily.

"That sounds accurate," interrupted the man darkly. "You have not been thinking. Do you not think gentlemen of your class frequent this place? Would you wish tittle tattle to rush around the *ton* that you were found in the arms of—"

"Yes, thank you, Alan," said Lawrence curtly.

Julia's head was whirling, she could hardly take in their words. Because he was right. It was shameless, what she had been doing, what she had wanted—and worse, she had done it in public.

Just because there had been no one there, that did not mean they were not seen...

"Julia?"

She blinked. Lawrence was standing before her, pulling a shirt on—most regrettably—but there was a soft kindness in his eyes that did not quite hide the desire still flaring in his pupils.

"Julia, I will see you soon," Lawrence muttered under his breath. "Soon. I promise you."

Julia glanced at the irate man behind him as happiness soared through her. Her mother, this man... no one would keep them apart.

"Soon."

CHAPTER NINE

February 14, 1810

"GOODNESS, LOOK AT him go!" Julia exclaimed, clapping with genuine astonishment at the way the two men before them were fighting. "I never saw the like!"

It wasn't supposed to be like this. Lawrence knew it, felt it in his blood. Knew his noble heritage should be balking at the very idea of allowing himself to spend time in this manner.

With this companion.

Yet they had fallen into the habit almost accidentally. *It was not his fault*, Lawrence told himself firmly. He tried not to permit his knee, thankfully encased in breeches, from touching the knee, regrettably covered by at least two layers of petticoats and a gown, of Julia.

He caught her eye and smiled weakly at her knowing look.

How did she do that? Immediately know precisely what he was thinking—worse, what he was fantasizing about?

Wishing that as they sat here on a bench supposedly watching a boxing match—not that he had paid any attention to the two poor blighters dashing each other to pieces—they were instead...

Well. Anywhere, but preferably alone. Alone, and with far fewer clothes than they were currently encumbered with.

"Penny for your thoughts?" Julia said quietly, so none of the rabble could hear her. "Or is that a little rich for your blood?"

Lawrence swallowed. It had been five days since he had lost all sense of self-control and permitted himself to touch Julia in a way he certainly should not have done.

Holding her in his arms. Allowing the pace of their punches to crowd out all sense, and instead focus on her warmth, the way her breath hitched as his hands came alongside hers...

And since then, almost every single day, they had been here. Together.

Never so close; oh no, that would never do. Lawrence was a gentleman—at least, he was technically undercover, but he knew himself to be a gentleman, even if these louts had no idea.

And a gentleman would not permit himself to lose all modesty in the face of a pretty woman. Probably.

"A little rich for my blood, yes," Lawrence said hoarsely. Julia grinned.

But she was not just a pretty woman, was she? Damn, he had met plenty of pretty women. Elegance and symmetry were all that was required for the title to be bestowed.

But real beauty—beauty of mind, of character, of something that could not be defined...

In short, he was lost. And he knew it.

"Do you not think them simply marvelous?" Julia breathed, her eyes agog as she watched the two men fight a closely matched battle.

"Yes," Lawrence said quietly. "Simply marvelous."

She flushed, as though she understood he was not merely speaking of the spectacle before them, but about the lady seated to his left.

In the days that had followed that rather scandalous moment when he had taught her how to fight—not that Lawrence ever wanted that woman near the end of a fist—their conversation had settled into something rather comfortable.

Comfortable! Lawrence could almost laugh, watching her silently as she gently accepted his attention while saying nothing.

Nothing about Julia was comfortable. Everything about her put him on edge, made him realize just how desperately he looked forward to these moments together, these snatched minutes, sometimes near an hour, when she could escape her commitments to Society and he could avoid Alan.

It was disgraceful. It was outrageous. It should be unthinkable.

Lawrence almost smiled. Whether as Lawrence Madgwick or Lawrence, Duke of Penshaw, he should not be having anything to do with a young lady who allowed herself to be kissed in Hyde Park or sneaked into boxing hells to watch working class men fight.

But Julia Dryden was not like other ladies.

A cheer, a shout, movement. Lawrence looked up at the ring. One of the men was holding his side, a hand up in the hope of respite. It was over.

Julia applauded loudly with the rest of the crowd. Lawrence managed to remember to bring his hands together as guilt seared through his chest.

He shouldn't be here.

At least, he should be here. Here, looking for a traitor, a murderer. So why did he find himself so easily distracted by this woman who appeared, most strangely, to consider him a man worthy of her time?

She knew hardly anything about him...

"Now, tell me," said Julia, leaning toward him and making Lawrence's stomach twist. "Why was it that the smaller man was able to get the better of him? I would have thought the greater the size, the greater the strength?"

Lawrence swallowed. If only that were true. He was half a head taller than Julia, and yet he was clay in her hands.

She saw him as a no one, a man with no fortune, no title, no skills or trade...and yet she did not judge him by that, and even if she did, it was a cover.

As her bright eyes fixed on his, a light smile dancing across her face, he knew Julia saw him as just a man. A man she evidently liked.

Lawrence tried to speak, found his voice a croak, and coughed to clear it. "Strength and size are not necessarily congruous."

Any other lady would have nodded politely, only have asked the question in an attempt to be polite.

But Julia was not like any other lady. Lawrence still felt he was only starting to scratch the surface of how Julia Dryden was different from all others, and he would rather like to remove the layers of clothing, too.

"Lawrence?"

"Right," he said hastily. *Now was not a time to lose all concentration. Perhaps he could skim the crowd looking for Mortimer while still talking to Julia...* "Strength. Size."

He was not so distracted that he did not catch the flush tinging her cheeks and found, to his great surprise, the color was undoubtedly reflected in his own.

Well, blast it. He hadn't meant it like that!

"What you have to know is that boxing is not purely about strength," Lawrence said, trying to keep his voice level. True, Julia seemed completely aware of what she did to him, but that didn't mean he had to broadcast it. "Strength is important, yes, but so is speed. Accuracy. Agility. Intelligence."

"Intelligence?" repeated Julia, surprise in her voice. "In boxing?"

Lawrence smiled as he watched her look back at the boxing ring. Yes, it was hard to believe there was any wit in a boxing match. From this distance, all one could see was cut and thrust, punches and groans, the spurt of blood if one received a particularly awkward uppercut.

"Intelligence," Lawrence affirmed. "Remember, you are making decisions at the rate of several a second, every second, for minutes at a time—and your health, your safety, your very body may depend on you making the correct decision."

Somehow, and he was not entirely sure how, Julia's hand had

slipped into his. It was a habit, amongst many, they really should be thinking of breaking, Lawrence thought happily as he curled his fingers around hers. Her pulse throbbed against his thumb. After all, it was outrageous.

Outrageously wonderful.

"And each of those decisions you make impacts the next," he said quietly as the crowd roared, the ring forgotten as Lawrence looked into Julia's eyes. *Could she understand what he was attempting to tell her?* "And the further into it you go, the fewer decisions you have. Everything leads up to one moment…one moment when you must decide whether to go left or right, to dodge or to weave, to duck or to lunge."

Julia's eyes were fixed on him as she leaned closer.

Lawrence tried to manage his breath. Tried to calm his fluttering heart. Tried not to think of—

Julia made it difficult to think straight. Much like a punch to the head or a bottle of his finest brandy from the Penshaw cellars…she was intoxicating.

"And then?" she said quietly. "When you have made your decision?"

Lawrence breathed out slowly, trying to smile. "Then you discover whether you were right."

The moment between them lasted far longer than was appropriate, but Lawrence knew they had left appropriate long ago.

Oh, if only they had met in a different way. If only they had met across a table, Lawrence thought wretchedly, *or at Almack's.* But then, would he have noticed her? It seemed impossible now, but as Duke of Penshaw, his family, his heritage already had a set. Families with titles as old and as dull as his own. Distant cousins, friends of his fathers, those he had attended university with.

Would he have even considered extending his circle, even for a pretty face? Would he have ever known the complexity and beauty of

Julia Dryden?

Julia sighed, then leaned her head against Lawrence's shoulder in a way that made his heart contract and his manhood strain against his breeches. "Well, whatever you decide, I am sure it will be the right decision."

Lawrence tried to swallow, throat dry. "Decision?"

He had not expected this, not so soon. Why, he was still attempting to decipher his feelings—his true feelings, beyond the desire—for Julia. He was still undercover. He was still trying to catch a traitor. Still trying to avenge his brother.

How could he make a decision about what he wanted for her, for them, now?

Julia nodded, her soft hair brushing against his cheek. "In your next boxing match."

Lawrence tried to nod as though he had known what she had meant all along.

Was it possible, he wondered, *that others had experienced this? That there were other gentlemen of his birth who found themselves enraptured with a lady who simply did not know of their status?*

His gaze drifted briefly over the fine eyelashes, bright pupils, delicate bow lips. Her cheeks high in color, her collarbone delicately visible even through the ties of her pelisse.

Lawrence's chest tightened. She saw him as nothing but a man with his fists and his wits...and yet she was here. With him. At the Almonry Den.

"Jules," he said quietly.

She smiled at the sound of her name on his lips. "Mmm?"

He hesitated. There was a delicate way to do this, the way a duke would, but he was free from those constraints now, wasn't he?

Besides, would she not be astonished to hear polite patter from his mouth when he was supposed to be undercover as a ruffian?

"Don't you have fancy balls and dinners to attend?"

The light disappeared from her eyes. "Yes."

Lawrence waited. A cheer went up around them, but he did not bother to look around.

No, he was far more intrigued by the woman beside him. A woman whose presence and touch was doing mightily unfortunate things to his loins.

"Well?" he prompted, as nothing more appeared forthcoming from Julia. "Why aren't you?"

"Hmm?"

Lawrence had to smile. It was rather gratifying, in a way, to see her so intoxicated by his presence, as he was in hers, that she could barely pay attention. "These balls, parties, and dinners, and all that. Why aren't you there? Why are you—"

"Here? With you?" Julia said the words Lawrence would rather not say.

He nodded, reveling in the way his cheek brushed up against her head still on his shoulder.

Sadly, she removed it as she fixed him with a more focused eye. "You mean, as a lady I should be out in Society, meeting with members of the *ton,* flattering the idiots I have the misfortune to meet, simpering at the eligible bachelors I am fortunate enough to get in their path, and hoping desperately to fall into a marriage that propels me one rung higher on the social ladder?"

Dear God, she was magnificent, Lawrence could not help but think. *Had anyone else put the marriage mart in better terms?*

At least, more accurate ones?

"Yes," he said with a half grin. "Something like that."

Julia laughed, rolling her eyes. "I am sorry, I did not mean to be so dismissive of my place... I know that there are many from the lower classes who would greatly wish—I should not have spoken so."

"No, I am glad you did," Lawrence said eagerly. Her hand was still in his. It should always be in his. "It is refreshing, I must say, to hear someone speak about Almack's and the like in such a straight-forward fashion."

Only too late did he spot the confusion in Julia's eyes. "What could you possibly know about Almack's?"

"Nothing," he said hastily. "Nothing at all."

He needed to distract her, Lawrence thought quickly. Something to cover the small blunder which had slipped from his tongue.

He did not want anyone to know of his true parentage, his rank, his duty.

Not until the duty he came here to perform was complete.

"One reads things—I read things," Lawrence said, seeing that Julia was not convinced. "Gossip, mostly."

An unknowable tension slipped from Julia's shoulders. "Ah, yes. Well, I cannot tell you what it is like to attend such places, hoping not to offend, hoping to catch the eye of the right people and not disgrace oneself so poorly that one ends up in those scandal sheets!"

I absolutely can, Lawrence thought darkly. And it was unpleasant indeed.

In fact, there had been a few scandals recently, now he came to think about it. All thanks to blatantly untrue gossip in the newspapers. Goodness knew where they were getting their information from, but it was always just close enough to the truth to end reputations, even if the eventual outcome was that the damned rag had to publish a retraction.

Not that they often did.

Julia sighed. "It can be... Well, a burden, I suppose. I know it is foolish to think of it in such terms when one has a roof over one's head, food and drink as one needs, and no real concerns over money..."

Her voice trailed away. Lawrence saw her discomfort and adored her for it.

Why, after all, she must think he envied her position in Society! Her rank, the class she had evidently been born to.

Perhaps if he was truly Lawrence Madgwick, fighting for coin each and every day in the hope of putting bread and a little paltry meat on the table, he would. As it was...

Lawrence slowly pushed a lock of Julia's hair behind her ear and tried not to concentrate on the feeling of her beneath his fingertips, the way her breath caught as he touched her. "Oh?"

"Oh," Julia said breathlessly, then collected herself. "Well, you fight each day to live your own life, on your own terms. You said before that you ran away from home, that you left the north."

It was not precisely what Lawrence had said, but he was hardly going to correct her. Not while her eyes fixed on him in that way, her fingers tightening in his grip, the warmth of her radiating into his side—

"You have to fight to get what you want," said Julia, her eyes not leaving his. "And I...I am fighting for what I want."

Her voice seemed to give way at that point, as though she knew she had gone too far and would only shame herself by continuing.

But Lawrence's curiosity was piqued. Here was a woman who had boldly approached him as he had lain beaten on the floor of a boxing ring. Who had kissed him most passionately. Who had stood in his arms mere days ago and almost cried out for his touch.

But she was going to halt now, just as she was about to reveal...

No. He had to know.

Lawrence was fast discovering his interest in Julia was not focused on her person. It was on her character, her presence, everything she was.

It was a worrying thought.

"Fight for what you want?" he nudged gently.

He watched Julia swallow, watched the war within her face as her forehead puckered. She wanted to speak, yet knew she should not.

He knew the feeling well.

Julia lifted her eyes to his boldly as a cheer went up around the

Almonry Den, another pair of fighters stepping undoubtedly into the boxing ring. "I have...oh, Lawrence, I should have told you before. Not that it's a secret, it's just... I have been given a deadline. By my mother. To be married."

Of all the things Lawrence expected to come from those lips, that was certainly not it.

"I have been given a deadline. By my mother. To be married."

His stomach jolted most painfully as her words echoed around his mind, a cacophony accompanied by the cheers and shouts of the crowd.

Married? Julia? Deadline—no, it was not possible.

"Your mother? A deadline?" Lawrence repeated.

He wanted to pull her close, into his arms and tell her that he would not permit it; that there was only one person she was going to marry, and that was—

Just before he thought those final words, Lawrence managed to pull himself back.

Dear Lord, he could not go down that path. Not now, as he waited for Mortimer to rear his ugly head. Perhaps not even then. He was a duke, after all.

"Yes, by my mother," Julia was saying awkwardly. "She says— well, that almost all those who came out into Society the same year I did are married, which is true, and that I have had plenty of admirers, which is also true—"

A spurt of bitter fire rose up in Lawrence's chest, so violently hot it threatened to burn not only him but all around him.

Admirers? Of Julia?

"—and so she has said if I am not engaged by Easter, she shall choose a husband for me and make all the necessary arrangements," Julia continued with a heavy sigh. "Not what I want, naturally, but..."

Her eyes had never left his. Lawrence was astonished to find he was now holding both of her hands in his. As though if he let go, there would be no possibility of finding her again, and the thought of losing her—

"Lawrence?"

"What?" he said distractedly, hardly knowing what he was doing.

Julia, married? To just anyone, anyone her mother could find?

It could not happen. It would not be allowed to happen.

Which was all very well, Lawrence thought wretchedly, but the trouble was he was hardly in a position to change the situation, was he?

He could not, would not return to Society until John Mortimer had been found. Blast it all, but he appeared to be no closer to finding the devil than when he had first arrived at the Almonry, months ago.

And even afterward...

Lawrence's jaw tightened. Even then, when he was returned to his title as Duke of Penshaw, what then? The estate would expect him to find a daughter of a duke, maybe an marquess's sister—at the very last, a woman from the line of earls.

Not a woman who dressed impeccably, snorted when she laughed, and had the brilliance of a diamond in her eyes but not around her neck.

"I shock you," said Julia quietly.

Lawrence's gaze sharpened. "No, I—"

"It offends you, perhaps, to hear of the upper classes doing such things," Julia said over the noise of the crowd. Another man had thudded to the floor of the boxing ring. "In your world, two people who love each other can choose each other, can be happy—but in my world..."

Lawrence swallowed. In his world, when he was able to leave his cover and return to it, he had even less choice than she did.

CHAPTER TEN

February 22, 1810

"**N**O! TRULY?"

"I swear on my honor," grinned Julia happily. "A full proposal, but in Latin."

She loved the way Lawrence snorted as they walked, arm in arm, back to the Almonry Den, a threat of snow drifting above their heads as the clouds grew heavier.

Lawrence was still laughing. "No, I am sorry, I do not believe it."

"Well believe it! I speak only the truth when I say that I did expect something of the sort," admitted Julia, grinning herself at the memory of the rather staid knight who had formally requested an audience with both her and her mother. "Some additional formality was to be assumed when it came to Sir Moses, he's such a stick in a mud, you have no idea."

For some strange reason, there was an odd smile across Lawrence's face as he ducked under a shop sign. "Oh, I am sure I can guess."

Julia's smile faltered. It was not a topic of conversation they frequented often, this distance between them.

She had become rather accustomed to an intimate closeness with Lawrence that would certainly have startled her mother. At times it made her heart race so wildly, it felt as though it was going to leap out of her chest and deposit itself in his hands…

But still. Though their conversation meandered in almost all directions, there was one that they ensured to keep away from.

The difference in their class.

Julia swallowed. *It was not so great, was it?* That was what she tried to convince herself whenever they were apart. Daydreaming about the way he had taught her to fight, wishing she was bold enough to kiss him again, indulging in fantastic imaginings of what it would be like…

Yet when they were together, it was painfully obvious. His clothes—it was a wonder they had lasted this far into the winter! His coarseness of expression, the way he could just say whatever he liked.

A privilege not extended to those of her breeding…

"Well, anyway," Julia said hastily, chasing away the thoughts troubling her mind. "He did not even get down on one knee, which I think outrageous—"

"Outrageous indeed," interjected Lawrence with a hint of mischief.

Julia thumped him none too gently on the arm. "Honestly, I cannot be the only romantic soul in London! Is there not a romantic thought in any man's head?"

When her gaze caught Lawrence's, she had to work hard not to flush, even though she may have been able to blame it on the blustery winter wind.

"My point is, he should have got down on one knee, and he should have at least pretended to have some sort of amour for me," Julia said with a laugh as they turned a corner, "and he should certainly not have proposed in Latin!"

They laughed as they waited on the edge of the pavement for a gap in the carriages so they could cross over.

"I cannot imagine it," Lawrence said, shaking his head. "Lord, the last time I heard Latin used in that way I—never mind."

He pulled her forward, stepping onto the road without as much as a look in either direction—but that did not matter. Julia was not looking at the road either.

She was looking at him.

Heard Latin used that way? When would a man of his birth have ever heard Latin in his life...unless, and the thought twisted her stomach most painfully and caused bitter bile to rise in her chest, unless he had been unfortunate enough to be imprisoned for something and taken to court...

Julia knew it was most uncouth of her, but as they stepped onto the next pavement and strode down the street on which the Almonry Den lay, she could not help but admit to herself that the thought of Lawrence being a criminal was rather...intriguing.

Intoxicating.

It added another layer of devilish excitement and scheming which she certainly should not be attracted to.

Julia's stomach lurched. *What a shame that she was.*

"Why are we hurrying back?" she asked, deciding they'd had quite enough talk of proposals.

But apparently, Lawrence did not agree. "And what reply did you give him?"

She blinked. "Give him?"

He nodded, pulling his threadbare coat a little closer and refusing, though it was surely a coincidence, to meet her eyes. "Sir Moses. What reply did you give?"

Julia's jaw dropped. *The very idea there could be any answer to such a question other than no...*

Prickles of discomfort drifted down her spine. How could Lawrence, of all people, think she would accept the hand of a man like that? When she spent so much of her time—all the time she could escape from her mother and her perpetual engagements—with him?

With the only man she had ever kissed. With the only man who made her feel—

"You didn't say yes, did you?"

The worried tone within Lawrence's voice quite put Julia's mind at ease.

She grinned as they arrived at the Almonry Den and stepped inside. "What would you say if I did?"

And it happened so swiftly that Julia gasped, all breath knocked from her lungs.

Lawrence had pushed her to the left, her feet scrabbling backward, and Julia's back hit the wall in the darkness of the unlit part of the Almonry Den. All she could do was gaze astonished up at the fierce face of the man who had pushed her there.

Lawrence. Who was now pushed up against her, his breathing heavy, his hands on her shoulders, pinning her against the wall—as though she would move.

As though Julia wanted to leave this spot.

As though she did not want to lean forward and accept his attentions. She could see, blazing in Lawrence's eyes, the need for her, the possessiveness surely sparked by—

"Sir Moses," Lawrence growled in a low voice, his eyes never wavering from hers, "is not about to be your husband."

Julia tried to breathe, she really did, but it was impossible as sparks of excitement and pleasure rushed through her body. Every part of her was tingling with the expectation of something she both knew and had never known before.

"No?" she breathed, trying to smile.

Lawrence leaned closer, his mouth only a few inches away, his gaze flickering to her lips then back to her eyes. "Not if I have anything to say about it."

Julia could not help it. She moaned, just under her breath, twisting under his forceful grip.

The shift of her hips brought them into contact with his own, brushing past his breeches as she was sure she felt—

"Ah, there you are, Lawrence—oh. I say."

Julia's eyes fluttered shut for a heartbeat, and in that instant, he released her. He was gone. It was as though it had not even happened.

"Alan, I was just coming to see you," said Lawrence smoothly.

With all the self-assuredness of an earl, Julia thought wildly. How did he do it? Be speaking to her of husbands, of men she should not marry, all crushed up against a wall...then lightly be discussing the next bout he was about to fight, quite happily, with Alan?

Julia tried to settle her skirts and pelisse without drawing too much attention from the older man, who had made it quite clear on numerous occasions that she was not welcome.

Not welcome. It would take a great deal more than that to keep her away.

"—not underestimate him," Alan was muttering, glancing at her as though she was purposefully overhearing their tactics to betray him to the enemy.

Julia raised her head and nodded imperiously at Alan, then immediately berated herself for such a thing. *Was she really going to become her mother?*

"—here soon, I am sure," Lawrence was saying in an undertone. "He cannot stay away much longer. He has been gone so—"

"He's there, isn't he?" interjected Julia lightly.

She had spoken to demonstrate she had been paying attention, that she was not here to distract Lawrence from his fights—far from it—but to encourage him.

Which did not explain why both Lawrence and Alan had such a surprising reaction to her pointing out that Tom was on the other side of the boxing ring.

Turning far more swiftly than she had thought the older man capable, Alan brought out a pistol, an actual pistol, from an inside pocket! Lawrence turned hastily, eyes wide, such furious anger in his eyes Julia had never seen before.

Vengeful. An anger beyond anything she had seen him possessed by.

Julia's mouth fell open as the two men rushed forward as though hastening into battle. *What was going on?*

Only a minute later, they had returned.

"You meant Tom," said Lawrence, a little sheepishly to Julia's eye.

She frowned. "Well of course I did—who else could I mean?"

If she was not very much mistaken, he glanced at Alan as though to prove he had been right all along, though about what, she could not tell.

"Hmmph," was the only reply Alan gave.

Julia discovered, much to her surprise, that her heart was beating rapidly, as though she had been the one to rush across the room and not them. "Why, what's wrong with him?"

"Do you know a man called John Mortimer?" Alan asked.

Julia blinked. *John Mortimer?* The name did not ring any bells, but then she had been trotted out and paraded before so many gentlemen over the last twelvemonth or so, it was difficult to recall.

"Mortimer?" she repeated.

The sound of the name caused a visible pain searing across Lawrence's face. Julia stared, but by the time she truly examined him, it was gone.

"Yes," said Lawrence, and there was a darkness, a suspicion to his voice she had never heard before. "Know the name?"

Julia shook her head slowly, her heart pattering painfully in her chest. *Why did this feel like a test?* "No, I don't. I don't think I've ever heard it before. Mortimer, did you say?"

He held her gaze only for a moment, then nodded. "Come on, Alan, I've got a match to fight."

But if Julia was not mistaken, Alan looked less happy with her answer.

"Hmmph," was the only response he made, but he gave her a look. It was discomfortingly similar to the look her mother gave her when she had been twisting the truth to her own ends.

"Lawrence, I—"

"Dear God, Julia! Not here again!"

Julia winced. She would know that irritating man's voice anywhere.

"How many times have I told you not to come here?" Donald said in a hiss as he stepped away from a pair of gentlemen and rushed over. "It is most outrageous that—"

"You have met Mr. Madgwick, I think, Donald?" Julia said as pleasantly as she could.

She had hoped…well, she was not entirely sure what she had hoped. A nod of recognition between the two men, perhaps. A handshake. Perhaps even a conversation.

Whatever she had hoped for, she did not receive. Donald barely glanced at the poorer man as though he did not exist, and instead grabbed Julia's sleeve and started pulling her away.

"You really shouldn't—"

"Donald, I know what I'm—"

"Lord, Dryden, is that your sister? What's she doing in a place like this?"

Donald closed his eyes in despair as he released Julia's sleeve, shaking his head before turning with a grin to his friends. "You know Julia, always looking for adventure!"

Heat seared Julia's cheeks—not because she was ashamed to have been found at the Almonry Den, but because it had caused such obvious pain to her brother.

She had embarrassed him.

Worse, he had attended the place with Mr. Rivers, the son of the haberdasher…and Mr. Lister. Two men of worse repute one could not find.

Not within the ranks of gentlemen, anyway.

"Ah, *Miss Dryden*," Mr. Lister said, his top lip sneering and revealing uneven teeth. "My word."

"Good on you, Miss, I don't see why the ladies cannot…I mean…yes," stumbled Mr. Rivers, evidently realizing—eventually—his words were not appropriate.

Julia sighed and tried to plaster a smile across her face.

A lady. A member of the ton.

Yes, it was all very well, but only since making Lawrence's acquaintance had she realized…well. How imprisoned she had become by her class. Her station in life.

Oh, to be like Lawrence! To be free to go where he wanted, do what he wanted, engage in sports and laugh and explore the city, no place too poor for him to wander. To be unrestricted by the rules of a Society that had no interest in a lady's pleasure. To lose himself in—

"Come on, Julia! Aren't you coming?"

Julia blinked. Donald was offering his arm, evidently cowed into accepting her presence by his friends, staring at her as though she had lost her wits.

She accepted his arm wordlessly, hardly able to cope with this ricochet of her brother's opinions, and allowed herself to be gently guided to a seat on the benches.

"And not a word of this to Mother," Donald hissed under his breath as the four of them sat down, his two friends arguing amiably about who they thought would win this next bout, Lawrence or Tom. "If she heard you were here—"

"I won't be the one to tell her, never fear," hissed back Julia, almost laughing at the ridiculous nature of his request. *Her, tell their mother that she had been at the Almonry Den?* "But your friends might—"

"I know, but it's your own damned fault for being found here, you know," said her brother as he nodded at a few men in the crowd. "What do you think you're doing here?"

Julia swallowed, her gaze drifting over the crowd—all of them men, naturally—until it settled on the boxing ring.

The boxing ring where Lawrence now stood. His expression was unreadable at this distance, but she could sense the tension in him. Something in the way he held himself, the rigidity of his shoulders.

What was she doing here?

She could not continue on this path with Lawrence, could she? Not without knowing...well. *Where it was going.*

Heat flushed her cheeks as both Lawrence and Tom stepped into the ring, to cheers and laughter as the latter almost tripped over the rope.

Lawrence was so evidently the favorite: taller, broader, stronger.

"Strength and size are not necessarily congruous."

Julia shivered, the memory of his words causing a ripple of delight across her chest. If they had been born from the same class, raised in the same circles...why, they could have been wed by now. Her mother would have had a polite yet discreet conversation, and it would have all been arranged with very little effort.

Married. To Lawrence. A shiver rushed through her.

But as it was...

"Go on, you big'un!" yelled Mr. Lister, a bright wildness in his eyes as he clung onto a scrap of paper. "I've got a guinea on him, you know."

"A guinea!" Mr. Rivers looked outraged. "On a single bout?"

A small smile crept across Julia's lips. She would have bet more than a guinea on him. After watching sufficient bouts, seeing Lawrence in the boxing ring with numerous opponents, she had a surer understanding of the thing now.

Tom would not stand a chance.

"How do you know the man, Miss Dryden?"

Julia glanced at Donald as Mr. Rivers asked what in any other situation would have been a simple question, and saw the panic in her brother's eyes.

She sighed. Lying was not a habit she had particularly wished to pick up, but it did not appear she had any choice. "I...I don't."

"I should think not," said Mr. Lister darkly. "A man like that, you can tell just to look at him that he's a rough sort."

The crush of his lips on hers, the way his soft hands became demanding as they pulled her closer...

Julia smiled, hugging the truth of the matter inside herself, the knowledge of Lawrence that no one else had. "I am sure he is."

The bell rang before any of them could utter another word, and the cacophony of the roaring crowd made it impossible to hear anything else.

Julia's heart raced with excitement as she watched Lawrence step neatly around Tom's first lunging attack, and knew just why so many people came here to watch such exciting entertainment.

The thrill of the chase, the tactics, the strength, the brutality, they all called to something within her she had never expected to find.

Or was it just that she so admired watching Lawrence's strong body dominate in the boxing ring, knowing its strength and power when it touched her own?

"A knockout would be my preference," Mr. Lister was saying. "But that Madgwick looks as mad as a dog..."

Julia glanced back to Lawrence and gasped as he took a terrible blow to the shoulder.

And that was when she knew. The knowledge was sudden, yes, but it was as though it had been there already, out of sight, hidden in the depths of her heart, waiting to be found...

She cared for him.

Julia's hands gripped together tightly in her lap as Mr. Lister roared and others booed, irritated their favorite had been the first to receive a blow. Their bets undoubtedly depended on it.

Yet the sensations roaring through Julia were far more than the hope of winning a little silver.

Lawrence was hurt. And that hurt her, a physical ache in her stomach that exploded in her chest and could not be contained.

She had to help him—save him, keep him safe, though what she could do—

Somehow Julia was standing on her feet. "Come on, Lawrence!"

Heads turned, as she knew they would, but she did not pay them any heed. Her full attention was affixed on Lawrence, her breathing tight in her chest, her hands still gripped together, as she shouted again.

"Go on, Lawrence!"

Just for a fraction of a second, he looked at her. She was sure their eyes met, and a sort of blazing determination shot from her to him.

Julia hardly took in the next three minutes. That it was three minutes she was informed later by Donald, irritated that he had bet the match would last a full ten, but at the time she could barely register a single second passing.

Lawrence won, of course. And when he rose triumphant, lifting his hands to accept the applause of the crowd, there was only one person he looked at.

Julia shivered with the intensity of his look, shared as it was in a room with hundreds.

It was for her.

The excitement filling her bones was nothing to do with the fight, at least not the one in the boxing ring. Julia had discovered how she felt about him, about this man who defied all conventions and would certainly be decried in her social circle...

And the battle against those feelings had been short indeed.

CHAPTER ELEVEN

L AWRENCE GROANED AS he raised his hand to his mouth. "Oh God, this bruise is going to ache forever!"

It was her laughter that revived him.

Lawrence watched, transfixed, as Julia laughed so hard she snorted. Whipping a hand to her mouth in horror as she realized the unladylike noise she had made, it only seemed to make her laugh worse.

"Oh, you'll survive," she said amiably, nudging him with her shoulder and making sparks of longing tingle down his arm. "It's only a bruise, after all."

Lawrence decided not to show her the terrible bruise that was already, just a few hours after the bout with Tom, starting to purple his side.

Partly because he did not want her sympathy. Well, fine, he wanted her sympathy, but not in that manner. He was no uncouth farmhand trying to impress a milkmaid. He was a duke.

No, Lawrence corrected himself ruefully. *He was undercover. His cover was that of a simple man.*

Partly because it would be rather unexpected for a man, let alone a gentleman in disguise, to start revealing his actual skin to a lady.

And partly because the locale where they were situated was not entirely set up for such intimacies.

Julia grinned happily as she took another bite of the pie Lawrence had insisted on treating her to after the fight. Her feet dangled over the side of the embankment just skimming the rather murky depths of the Thames.

"A fine idea, this," she said happily.

Lawrence could not help but smile in return. It was. Hot, steaming pork pies, the pastry absolutely coated with grease, eaten side by side as they sat on the bank of the Thames as they watched the world go by.

It was a simple pleasure he had never been afforded when in town under his true name. Eating a pie from a street seller? His father would have turned in his grave.

Yet the enticing smells had always intrigued Lawrence, and now, finally, he was able to taste their delights.

They weren't the only delights he wanted to taste...

"Your brother didn't wish to join us?" he asked lightly.

At least, as lightly as he could manage. Lawrence wasn't sure whether his curiosity had been audible in his question, but he had to know.

Julia rolled her eyes as she swallowed another mouthful. "Donald, eat something that wasn't prepared at his club, a Society dinner, or Cook at home? Never fear."

She took another bite happily as Lawrence marveled.

Well, it was difficult not to. He had never encountered a woman of her breeding who would have done this. She was happily sat with a gentleman—a *man*, moreover, who was not a relative, in plain sight of the whole world.

Of the docks, no less.

Something painful stirred in his chest that had nothing to do with the successful bout he had just won at the Almonry. The Almonry Den he should still, technically, be in. How else would he find Mortimer?

Memories of a rather awkward conversation, just after he had leveled Tom to the floor, echoed in Lawrence's mind.

"And you truly trust her?" Alan had said darkly.

"With my life," Lawrence had replied, only discovering the fierce veracity of his words as he spoke. "I trust Julia Dryden, Alan, and I don't understand why you—"

"Because she has beguiled you, that's why," the older man had said heavily. "Because she has become the only thing you think about, the only person you wish to see. A complete distraction from the whole purpose of us being here!"

And Lawrence had opened his mouth to argue, to disdainfully prove the man utterly wrong. Then shut his mouth.

Well, what could he say? Every accusation was true. She had beguiled him, body and soul. He longed for these moments they could spend together. She was the only person he wanted to see, when fighting in the ring but also when outside it.

And she had proven to be a most excellent distraction from finding John Mortimer.

Lawrence looked askance at the woman beside him. Julia was carefully trying to lick a crumb of flaky pastry from her lips, utterly ignoring the world around her. When she captured it, her eyes fluttered shut with the unadulterated pleasure of the flavor.

His loins lurched. *Dear God, what a distraction.*

But if Alan was right…

"—too much of a coincidence," his mentor had said firmly. "You think a lady of her breeding would be interested in you?"

"I am the Duke of—"

"Not to her," Alan had said darkly. "To her, you're just a man who fights and lives in a hovel. Two rooms of a slum. You think she would actually be interested in you, seek you out, if she did not have an ulterior motive?" When Lawrence did not reply, he pressed his point. "If she was not *working for Mortimer?*"

The happiness always present in his heart whenever Lawrence was with Julia flickered for a moment. The thought that she could in some way be connected to Mortimer…worse, that she could be purposefully distracting him from—

"I am impressed, you know."

Lawrence blinked. "You are?"

Julia nodded, wintery sunlight illuminating her hair. "Yes. I thought for an instant that you may struggle to beat that Tom again, but you did well."

He could not help but smile, all fears she was working against him fading like frost in the morning sun. "Your encouragement was what did it."

The intention had not been to embarrass her, but a gentle flush tinged her cheeks. "Oh. You heard."

Heard? Of course, I heard, Lawrence wanted to say. *You think a single word could slip from your lips without me paying it heed? You think every breath is not noted, that every moment I wish I could stop that breath with a kiss—*

"Well, it was a crowded place and much excitement abounded at your fight," Julia said with a laugh. "You owe my brother an apology, though."

Lawrence stiffened. *An apology, for her brother?*

The only other time a brother had demanded an apology, a rather unfortunate duel had taken place. He had aimed to miss, of course. It wasn't his fault the fool stepped to the left.

Guildford's ear would never be the same.

"He bet your fight would last at least ten minutes," said Julia conversationally, utterly ignorant of the thoughts rushing through Lawrence's mind. "And lost a shilling, which he would not stop muttering about, the fool."

Lawrence forced his shoulders to relax. She thought him no more than a poor man with a desire to live life on his own terms, he reminded himself. A man with no income and little manners.

Only half of that was true…

"Well, you can apologize to your brother for me," Lawrence said aloud.

"Oh. I thought...you might wish to speak with him."

He glanced at Julia whose gaze had dropped to her hands, now empty of pie.

Was that disappointment in her voice...but that would make no sense. Why would Julia wish him to speak to her brother?

And then a horrible and yet wonderful thought struck him. Brother, mother, yes, Julia had mentioned both. But no father. And that would mean—

"Well, I am sure Donald will win back that shilling somehow," Julia said brightly, as though there had been no moment between them, no shimmering potential future. "He seems to be continually at the Old Duke's—that's a gaming hell, just off—"

"Yes, I know it," said Lawrence without thinking.

Julia's eyebrow raised.

Damn. Damn, damn, and blast it to hell!

Seven months, more, he had managed to concoct a life that was never given a second glance...and Julia had threatened to unravel it.

Lawrence tried to concentrate, tried not to become distracted by the beauty of the woman beside him, but it was a damned hard job.

"Thank you for coming with me," said Lawrence quietly. "Here, I mean."

Julia looked around, eyes eager. "You know, I've never been here."

"That, I can well believe."

"Not a place for someone of my stock, as my mother would say," she said darkly, distaste quite evident on her tongue.

Lawrence stifled a laugh. Even without meeting the aforementioned Mrs. Dryden, he had met enough Society mamas to know precisely the sort of tone of Julia's mother.

One that, perhaps, he would have taken.

It was a strange thought, but Lawrence had to admit he had believed he knew much of the world before he had entered this particular sphere, only to discover to his great surprise that he knew very little.

Without Alan to guide him …well. He would have revealed himself immediately.

"I like it down here," Lawrence said quietly, the moment drawing honesty from him. Truth he should probably have fought against. "The water, I mean."

A mere look at Julia made him laugh.

"Not with any intentions to dive into it or, God forbid, drink it," he chuckled ruefully. "Not if I want to be well enough to fight another bout. No, I meant…well. Being near water. It calms me, somehow. I never thought about it much when I lived at Pen—up in the north."

Cursing himself for his own stupidity, Lawrence could only hope Julia had not noticed his slip.

"Pen?" Julia said curiously, the skirts of gown whipping in the growing wind, echoing the noise of the sails of the ships before them. "Is that where you grew up?"

Lawrence swallowed. *Penshaw Place.* He had thought for a while, when a small child, that Penshaw Place was the entire world. It was large enough for a child to get good and lost in, after all. Hundreds of acres of woodland, moors, farmland, a few villages, even a town.

And that was after one found their way out of the ornamental gardens, the lake, and the deer park.

Strange. One never seemed to value the place when one was there. It had become a sort of prison, Lawrence supposed, though he had never consciously thought of it that way when there. But the staidness, the routine, the level of respectability one had to maintain all the time. Always ensuring no one ever saw him crack a smile or admit an opinion—

"You've gone again."

Lawrence started. "What?"

Julia was smiling wistfully. "Whenever you think of the north, where you came from—I will not call it home, for you do not—you are always overcome by…something. Not melancholy. But not something far from it."

He swallowed. That was the trouble with a perceptive woman. They spoke truth to you that you believed you had hidden, hidden well.

And yet apparently it was quite evident from his face, unfortunately.

"My home…my home is not where it was," Lawrence found himself saying.

It was not a thought he'd had before, but now he said it, the truth was quite evident.

Home was where Julia was.

A shiver of heat, a rush of desire, an ache he knew could never be fulfilled claimed his bones. Lawrence abandoned himself to the feelings, just for a moment.

Then he tried to pull himself together. *This was madness!* He had a job to do, unusual for most dukes. But he had volunteered for it, the moment the news of his brother's death had been brought to Penshaw Place, and he was not about to abandon it for—

Julia's hand slipped into his own. "You don't have to talk about it. I know it pains you."

Lawrence's heart skipped a beat. There was such softness in her, such kindness, and yet such strength, such resilience. Had ever these two opposites met so perfectly?

"I always thought, once I left Pen—where I was born," Lawrence said slowly, only just catching the repeat of his initial mistake, and thanking the heavens he had not completed the word, "that I would return there. That I would…fight my way back there, I suppose."

He laughed at the thought. Julia's fingers squeezed his. They gave him the courage, courage he had not realized he needed, to continue.

"Yet I think it was only when I left that I could look back on it with any sort of—well, clarity!" Lawrence smiled, and Julia met it with one of her own. "Does that make sense?"

"Not in the slightest," she said cheerfully.

Lawrence's face fell. "What?"

"Well, there's so much about you that I don't know," Julia said pointedly, though there was no malice in her words. "It's your own business, naturally, and I would not wish to pry, but... Lawrence, you fascinate me."

Her words were untamed, her tone unrestrained, and Lawrence's heart pounded painfully as he tried to look away.

He fascinated her?

Dear God, it was nothing to his curiosity about her. How had he managed to suffer four Seasons in London—he had managed to spend most of the last few years in the north, pleading responsibilities he had pretended or just made up—without being captivated by her?

Without knowing, without a shadow of a doubt, that he loved—

"You are far more fascinating," Lawrence said in a low voice.

Julia smiled, her gaze dropping to her hands—hands that were entangled with his own. "If you were a gentleman, I would ask what your intentions were."

Lawrence bit his lip as a shout echoed down the docks.

If he was acting the gentleman, he would have made them clear by now to her father, if he lived, or her brother.

But he was not. His cover would not permit such niceties, and he could not trust anyone else with the secret of his true identity until the blaggard was caught.

And who knew when that would be?

"If I were a...a gentleman," he said quietly, the words feeling strange on his lips, "I would tell you."

She laughed, and a spark of teasing happiness fired through Lawrence's chest. "I suppose I deserved that."

"Honestly, Jules, if I knew what my own plans were for the next year—the next six months, the next week, I would tell you," Lawrence said urgently, the need for her to believe him billowing in his chest. "But I don't know. I cannot tell you."

Until John Mortimer is dead or caught, Lawrence was starting to realize, everything he wanted for himself, for Julia...well, it would have to wait.

Wait until the man was found and his own true identity could be revealed.

Only now did Lawrence realize what a trap he had laid. The rest of his life stretched out before him, empty, devoid of anything save John Mortimer. He could neither commit to Julia nor reply to any of the urgent letters his sister had sent to his rooms at the Dulverton Club, sent on by Alan.

"But if you could," Julia said quietly, "dictate your fate, I mean. What would you do?"

Lawrence swallowed. He should not say it. *He should not—*"That would depend."

"On what?"

He should not—"On you."

Her eyes widened. "On—on me?"

Lawrence nodded, unable to tear his gaze away, knowing if he had his own way, they would leave this place, return to his rooms, and—

"Lawrence," Julia breathed.

Somehow, he had lifted a hand to her cheek, turning her face toward him. His head lowering, slowly, inch by painful inch. Julia's lips parted, she wanted this, wanted this kiss, wanted him—

And Lawrence knew if he kissed her now, if he lost himself in the heady temptation Julia did not even know she offered, he would have to do it. He would offer marriage.

And then what would she do? The elegant young lady, part of the *ton* and Almack's voucher holder...would she accept the hand of a poor fighter who lived in two rooms?

Lawrence would never know. Twisting to lean into him, Julia's eyes widened in horror as she suddenly lost her balance and plummeted four feet down into the Thames.

"Jules!"

She floated, which was a relief. Lawrence was no expert in these matters, but it appeared sufficient air was entrapped within her billowing skirts to provide her with the necessary buoyancy to—

"L-Lawrence!" Julia spluttered, trying simultaneously to brush the water out of her eyes, not consume any of the Thames, and glare up at him as he tried not to laugh. "Get me out of here!"

Lawrence kneeled down and heaved. A sopping wet, slightly irate, and glaring Julia emerged.

"They are laughing at me," said Julia stiffly, trying to ring out water from her bonnet, which had somehow managed to remain on her head.

He glanced up. She was correct. The dockhands had found the entire adventure rather amusing. It was quite funny from up here, Lawrence thought, though he knew better than to remark on this.

"You'll freeze," he said instead, drawing an arm around her and wishing he could warm her up in quite a different manner. "Come on, I'll find you a carriage."

"I d-don't n-need a—"

"Yes, you do," Lawrence said firmly. *Why was it that the woman was always so obstinate?* "Come on."

Julia grinned as they reached a street whereupon two carriages were loitering, their drivers sharing a measly cigar that looked to Lawrence's eyes to have been constructed of odds and ends.

"You were about to kiss me."

"I was indeed," admitted Lawrence ruefully. "That'll teach me to attempt romance by the Thames."

"I would take romance from you anywhere," Julia whispered.

He tried not to think about stripping off all those wet things and taking her to such heights of pleasure she had never known. "Flattery will get you nowhere."

She laughed as Lawrence nodded at one of the men who immediately handed over his cigar to his companion and strode over. "Not where I want. Not with you."

Lawrence's stomach lurched. She did not know what she was saying; or if she did, she was doubtless giddy from the fall.

Or, a third and more delectable option, she knew precisely what she was saying...

"Home with you," Lawrence said, wishing to goodness he had fewer morals and better digs. A better bed. "Off with your wet things as soon as you get in, and—"

"Care to come with me?"

Lawrence's jaw tightened, but he shook his head with a wry smile as Julia settled into the carriage. "You're a temptress, Julia Dryden."

She grinned mischievously as the driver mounted and clicked at the horses. "Not enough, it seems."

CHAPTER TWELVE

February 28, 1810

"YOU'RE OUT OF your wits," Lawrence said sternly.

Julia grinned, almost fizzing with excitement. "I assure you, I am perfectly sane."

The idea was a perfect one, and she could not understand why the tall man before her was not immediately convinced.

It had come to her in the night, and after gaining Donald's support—that was, after arguing with him for five minutes, threatening him for five, and finally offering to loan him the twenty pounds he had been asking for, which she knew she would never see again—she had come straight to the Almonry Den.

To see him.

Lawrence pulled a hand through his hair with the air of a man driven beyond distraction. "Julia, you cannot seriously—"

"It is already arranged," she interrupted, almost singing with happiness. "You are to arrive at seven o'clock."

"But—Julia, the last thing your mother is going to want to do is meet me!" Lawrence said heavily, almost laughing at her excitement. "She's trying to marry you off, not degrade you with my company! Dear God, why would you invite me to dinner?"

Because, Julia wanted to say, *I am tired of having my two worlds entire-*

ly separate. Because my mother won't be able to stop herself liking you, once she has met you. Because if I truly wish to…if I want to one day…

Well. Then you will have to be introduced to my mother. That's all.

None of these frantic thoughts whirling through Julia's mind were uttered, of course. That would be much too forward.

She almost laughed. *Too forward?* Every one of her interactions with Lawrence Madgwick was too forward. She was so forward, she was almost leaping on—

"Absolutely not," said Lawrence firmly.

All the excitement flooded out of Julia as her shoulders sagged. "You…you mean you won't come?"

It had all seemed so perfect. Her mother had suggested a quiet evening, just a few guests for dinner, and had asked Julia if she had anyone in mind.

And there was only one person on her mind at the moment.

"Lawrence Madgwick," she had said to Donald's general astonishment from across the breakfast table that morning. "I would like to invite Law—Mr. Madgwick."

Try as he might, Donald had been unable to make her take back the words, though he had waggled his eyebrows most expressively over the teapot.

"Mr. Madgwick?" Mrs. Dryden had wrinkled her nose at the unfamiliar name. "Is he one of Lady Romeril's proteges?"

"No," said Julia eventually. It would have been a convenient lie, to be sure, and her mother would merely have accepted it immediately…but there was too great a chance that Lady Romeril herself would hear of it.

She would not face Lady Romeril unless absolutely backed into a corner. Which was typically how anyone found themselves facing Lady Romeril, now she came to think about it.

"Well?" Her mother had raised an eyebrow. "How do you know

him, then?"

Julia had cast about for an answer that was as far away from "I saw him fighting an illegal boxing match at Almonry, which Don took me to, and I have been unable to extricate myself from him ever since" as possible.

"He's a friend of Donald's," she had said weakly.

Donald had choked on his poached egg and potatoes.

"Of Donald?" repeated their mother suspiciously. "I have never heard of—"

"That is because—" Donald started darkly. "Ouch!"

Julia glared at her younger brother. Her kick had been well aimed, and it could be repeated, her look tried to communicate.

Evidently her silent expression had worked.

"A friend of Donald's," said Donald weakly. "I mean, of mine. Yes."

Their mother had looked between them suspiciously, but there was no use. She had offered them each an invitation. "Fine. This Mr. Madgwick, and one of your friends, Donald—or even better, a young lady..."

Julia grinned up at Lawrence. She had found him in his rooms—not that she had been so brazen as to go up to them, obviously. She was no harlot. She may be in her imagination, but not in actuality.

Not for lack of trying. She had really thought the dip in the Thames would have convinced him, pushed him over the edge, as it were.

She had heard Donald and his friends talking once before about the allure of a woman in a sheer gown, and she had purposefully worn a white one in the hopes of enticing Lawrence if she could expertly fall into the Thames. It had all gone so well.

It wasn't her fault the damned thing was so cold.

"Your mother," Lawrence said warily. "Your mother. Has invited me. To dinner."

Julia beamed. "Yes. Almost. In a way—"

"Jules," Lawrence warned, his voice low.

All she could do was beam. He was still a little sweaty from the boxing ring, his fringe slightly damp, a heady scent rising from him like the most potent aphrodisiac ever invented.

If only they were not still standing in full view of a dissipating crowd. The afternoon's entertainment was over. Only when evening came would they return to...

And Julia's heart sank. "Oh. Of course, I did not think. You...you will be fighting this evening, won't you?"

How could she not have thought of it? As guilt and shame colored her cheeks and tensed her fingers now clasped together before her, Julia knew precisely why she had not.

Because she was unaccustomed to the limitations of a profession. If one could call this a profession, which her mother certainly would not.

Every time she attempted to demonstrate to Lawrence that she accepted him for what, for who he was, she managed to stumble into a blunder!

A gentle hand tipped up her chin so she was looking once more into the handsome visage of Lawrence.

"You forgot," he said gently.

Julia swallowed. "I so wanted you to come to dinner."

She had not intended to plead. It was not her way. If Lawrence did not want to come, that was different from being unable to—

Lawrence sighed. "Who else will be there?"

Was it not enough that she would be there? "My mother, my brother, myself, and a Miss Banfield. I have met her a few times, I think my brother is fond of her."

"And that's all?"

Julia could not comprehend the anxiety the guestlist appeared to be causing Lawrence. *What did it matter?* "That is all."

He hesitated for a few moments longer, a strange look of indecision on his face. Then finally, "Seven o'clock?"

A small sliver of hope shone. "Seven o'clock."

Julia watched as he glanced away and caught the eye of his friend, the older man who was always with him. She saw something strange between them. A strange sort of silent request for permission.

It was difficult not to glare at the man as he hesitated. *What sort of hold did this Alan have over Lawrence?* She had never asked, had learned swiftly Lawrence was not the sort of man to answer questions, but still. That did not cease her curiosity.

Only when the man gave a sigh, then a nod before turning away from them both, did Julia relax.

"Perfect," she said brightly. "In fact, it might be worth you turning up at six o'clock, at the side door. My brother will be leaving a jacket and—"

"I may not have received an invitation to dine at Mayfair before," said Lawrence with something like a smile on his lips, "but I know how to dress."

Julia hesitated. *Of course, he knew how gentlemen dressed; one saw them all the time, but she had assumed...well. That he would not have the apparel of the breeding her mother would expect—*

"Seven o'clock then," Lawrence sighed ruefully with a laugh. "God help us all."

The next few hours of the day whirled by so swiftly, it felt like no time at all that seven o'clock was chiming from all the clocks in the Dryden house.

Donald looked up from where he was standing by the fire in the drawing room. "Your Mr. Madgwick is late."

Julia snorted. "Nonsense."

"I heard the chimes myself!"

"Your Miss Banfield isn't here," Julia pointed out, trying to keep her voice level so their mother would not look up from her embroidery at the hissed conversation.

Donald rolled his eyes. "Ladies are supposed to be fashionably late, it would not do for her to be here on the dot, but your—"

From somewhere along the hall, a bell jangled. Normally this would do nothing to Julia's sensibilities. She heard the doorbell go every day, after all. But not tonight. Tonight was different.

Heart pounding painfully in her chest, every nerve heightened, Julia forced herself to remain seated as a pair of footsteps sounded along the hall. Two pairs of footsteps.

When the door opened, Julia rose politely. It was fortunate indeed her mother took upon herself the responsibility of welcoming their first guest, as Julia was not certain whether her voice would have sounded.

Lawrence Madgwick.

There he stood, tall, dashing, in a pair of breeches and jacket that would not have looked out of place at Almack's or St. James's Court, looking every inch the gentleman. He had pomaded his hair, there was a slightly battered yet serviceable pocket watch dangling from a chain, and he was the utter picture of respectability.

Julia's breath caught in her throat, and warmth pooled between her legs. She had thought him handsome as he was, in clothing that needed seeing to, and of course he had been. He was.

But seeing him here, dressed in finery as though he was about to dance with her...

"—delighted to make your acquaintance, Mrs. Dryden," Lawrence was saying smoothly, bowing just as a gentleman ought, then inclining his head to Donald, who had not stepped away from the fireplace. "Such an honor."

Julia watched in astonishment as her mother preened, murmuring genteel gratitude. *Well!* She had thought her mother would be impressed with Lawrence but had not expected... expected him to turn out so well.

She flushed at the thought, for it was not particularly kind. The thing was, she had wondered, worried even that she may have to explain away a few peculiarities of manner or attire, particularly as he insisted in finding his own.

Where on earth had he found such elegant clothes?

"Ah, Miss Dryden."

Julia blinked. Somehow, she was not sure how, Lawrence had managed to traverse the eternity that was the drawing room floor. "Lawrence."

Lawrence's eyes sparkled. "Mr. Madgwick, if you do not mind, for this evening."

He breathed the words, a glint mischief in his eye that made Julia grin.

Well, they had managed it so far, tricking her mother that the man before her was no prizefighter but instead a gentleman of the highest order. The trouble was, would he similarly impress Miss Banfield? Would he be able to maintain the charade for the entire evening?

"Ah, what a shame."

Julia's ears pricked at her mother's words. "What's a shame?"

Mrs. Dryden was passing a notecard to Donald. "Miss Banfield. She has taken a chill and so will be unable to attend tonight. Such a shame."

Julia swallowed. "How unfortunate."

Unfortunate? It was glorious. Though she had met the poor Miss Banfield, as she would undoubtedly be described by her mother for the rest of the evening, only a few times, Julia had remarked on her pretty expression and elegant figure.

Not, now she came to think of it, a woman she wanted to dangle under Lawrence's nose.

Not that he would look at anyone else. Julia shivered as his intense gaze returned to her. No, he would do no such thing.

"How very sad for Miss Banfield," said Lawrence with a slight smile. "I know how easily a young lady can catch a chill in London during the winter."

Heat scalded Julia's cheeks, and she looked away in the hope of not revealing herself. Though she could not be sure, she was convinced Lawrence was recalling a few words that had slipped out from her lustful mouth just days ago.

"You're a temptress, Julia Dryden."

"Not enough, it seems."

Well, she could not help it. Who could when looking at Lawrence?

"Shall we go through?"

Julia blinked. Lawrence had asked something, but the words had not made sense. "Go where?"

He was holding out his arm, a smile on his lips. "Through. I assume the gong means that dinner is served?"

Looking about wildly, Julia saw to her surprise that the gong must have been rung. There was no other reason for her mother to be putting down her embroidery and accepting Donald's arm.

"You did not hear it?"

She shook her head with a laugh at Lawrence's question. "No! No, I must have been...distracted."

When she met his gaze, she knew he understood; that he was the distraction, the one making it impossible to concentrate. Was she having such an effect on him? Was it possible the heat she felt between them was not only emanating from her, but—

"Julia! Really, your manners, girl!"

"Yes, yes, right," Julia said hastily, grabbing Lawrence's arm and striding forward. "Sorry, Mama."

Excited tingles curling between her collarbones, between her breasts, and lingering downward overcame her senses at being so close to Lawrence—and in her own home, too!—but this pleasantness gave way to horror as they entered the dining table.

Oh, Mama! Julia was not foolish enough to exclaim aloud, but if she could have done, her tone would have dripped with disappointment.

It was always the way with their mother. Whenever a new guest came to dine at the Drydens...well. She had to make a spectacle of them, didn't she?

Julia stared, crestfallen, at the complexity of dining apparatus her mother had evidently instructed the housekeeper to have laid out. More forks than one could shake a stick at, a complicated sort of knife that looked, her heart sinking, like the implement used to remove snails or oysters from their shells, and four spoons. *Four! What on earth could they need four spoons for!*

Donald stifled a laugh as he sat down. Julia glared, wishing she was seated opposite him so that she could give him a fine kick.

But as it was, her mother had contrived to place her beside her brother and opposite Lawrence.

It was on the tip of her tongue to request a change of seating, but as Lawrence helped her into a chair, a shiver rushing down her arms as his breath gently warmed them, Julia knew it would do no good. Her mother would only ask questions.

Questions she certainly was not going to answer.

"Well, isn't this nice?" Mrs. Dryden said brightly. "A nice informal dinner."

Julia rolled her eyes. *Well, really!* Her mother was always trying to impress, always hopeful a gentleman at her table would take a liking to her daughter... and that her daughter would take a liking to the gentleman.

The trouble was, Lawrence did not need to be impressed. Why, his two rooms alone would probably fit in this room! And now he was faced with—

"Ah, we are having oysters, then?" Lawrence said smoothly, permitting the Drydens' only footman to place his napkin on his lap. "From Whitstable, I trust? I hear the best oysters have to be sourced from Whitstable."

Julia tried to prevent her jaw from falling as Lawrence and her mother entered a lively, yet respectable debate about the best seaside town to purchase oysters from—her mother favoring, Brighton, far more fashionable.

This could not be happening.

At least, it was happening, and she had no idea how.

"—simply must visit Whitstable, not only for the oysters but for, and do forgive me Mrs. Dryden, but for the bathing," Lawrence was saying most cheerfully as quail eggs were brought through for the next course. He nonchalantly cracked them with one spoon and scooped them out with a second. "Most invigorating and excellent for the feminine health."

Julia's mouth was open. She attempted to cover up her inelegance by shoveling a mouthful of food inside it. Then she choked. She had spooned in an entire quail's egg, shell and all.

"—delightful to hear a gentleman converse on the subject of the feminine health," her mother was saying, clearly charmed. "Why, I have told Julia if I have told her a thousand times, it is imperative she prevents any hint of a chill…"

Julia flushed into her napkin as she attempted to hide her face at such words.

How was this happening? If she'd had any forethought, she would have armed Lawrence with the three safest topics to discuss with her mother: the weather, the importance of loyalty to His Majesty, and the dearth of good silk. That would have been that.

The evening would have been dull, to be sure, but it would have been safe.

This was unprecedented. How did a man who earned a living by his fists know where to get the best oysters from? Or that Whitstable had bathing? Or, as she listened in part horror, part glee at their continuing conversation, that Mozart was best when listened to in the evening, but Bach better in the morning?

"It is all about resonance," Lawrence was saying airily, ignoring the footman as was expected by a gentleman as his plate was removed and the next course, a complicated sort of roast chicken with vegetables to be served by platter, brought through. "Bach's tonal choices, as I am sure you know, Mrs. Dryden, are such that—"

"How on earth did you quiz him on all this?" muttered Donald beside her.

Julia stared at her brother, then back to the man she was fast realizing she could not spend her life without. "I...I have no idea."

It seemed safer to say nothing. As the meal progressed, Julia recovered herself enough to partake in the conversation—at least, to attempt to—but each passing moment offered her a fresh opportunity to marvel at Lawrence.

His cover—that he was a gentleman of the north, infrequently in London—appeared to be perfect. She could not fault him, not in the way he held his wine glass, by the stem as it was white, nor how he bowed deeply to them both she and her mother withdrew, nor how charmingly he played the pianoforte when the men joined them.

Julia swallowed, hardly daring to breathe in case the mirage of the gentleman Lawrence disappeared.

"Well, I must say," said her mother in a low voice approvingly as Donald rang the bell for Lawrence's greatcoat and hat to be retrieved at the end of the evening. "I was a little concerned when I had not heard of your acquaintance, Julia, but I am delighted to find him a gentleman."

Julia almost laughed. "Yes. Yes, so am I."

"And I must presume," continued her mother with a knowing look in her eyes, "you only requested his presence tonight because you believe he will soon make an offer of—"

"Mr. Madgwick," Julia said, rising hastily and stepping away from her mother, hoping the topic of conversation could not be read on her cheeks. "Let me see you to the door."

"Really, Julia," came her mother's cry of astonishment. "It is for the servants to—"

"It's no trouble," Julia interrupted. "Come on, Mr. Madgwick, let's see if we can find where the housekeeper has hidden your hat."

Only when the two of them had stepped out of the drawing room—Lawrence having bowed very elegantly to her mother and nodded again to Donald—did Julia's shoulders slump, and she punched Lawrence as hard as she could in the arm.

"Ouch!"

"You deserve it," she hissed as they walked down the corridor toward the hallway. "After all that talk—"

"Did you like it?" Lawrence grinned, his cheeks slightly flushed from the excitement, Julia presumed, of success. "I thought it would impress your mother the most when I—"

"And here I was, worried you would stick out like a sore thumb!" Julia said with a laugh, though she stifled it when they reached the hallway and saw their housekeeper waiting with greatcoat and hat. "Thank you, that will be all."

If the servant was astonished that the daughter of the house was going to permit herself to be alone, albeit briefly, with a gentleman, she said nothing.

The door closed. Julia took a deep breath. They were alone.

"You were magnificent," she said.

Lawrence, but not Lawrence. A Lawrence in formal attire, in the getup of a gentleman. Even as he pulled on the greatcoat and placed the hat above his head, they did not detract but merely added to the overall image.

An image that was having a mighty effect on her.

"You are pleased?"

"This whole evening, you, you went far beyond what I expected. Why, you could have almost been a duke, the way you spoke to my mother!"

She laughed and expected him to join her, but for some reason, Lawrence's smile was perfunctory.

"Yes. Yes, I suppose so."

"But where did you learn it all?" Julia asked eagerly. There was still so much about Lawrence she did not know, so much she wanted to learn.

Only then did she notice her eagerness had taken her forward, only a foot away from him.

"I was…taught," Lawrence said slowly. "Is that not how everyone learns anything?"

"Yes, but…well, surely you could not have learned all that in just a few hours?" pointed out Julia. "I mean, all those spoons!"

"I was taught not today, but years ago. By…by a duke, as a matter of fact."

Julia stared. *The life this man must have led…to be fighting for his very livelihood in London, but to have spent time in the company of a duke!*

"A duke? No—a duke? What duke?" she demanded.

A teasing smile crept across Lawrence's face. "Never you mind."

"But I do mind." Julia stepped forward, unable to help herself. This man, this mystery, this enticement. Would she ever be free of him now that she knew so much and yet so little? "Lawrence, I—"

She was unable to continue. Not that she minded. Lawrence had leaned down, bestowing at first a reverent and then a most irreverent kiss on her lips.

Julia moaned, immediately throwing her arms around his neck and pulling him close. This was what she had wanted, what she had dreamed of. Herself in his arms, Lawrence's mouth on hers, his fingers around her waist. The strength of his grip told her in no uncertain terms that he had wanted this just as long, perhaps longer, than she had.

Tingles of explosive pleasure shot down her body, every sensation heightened, and Julia whimpered with delight as Lawrence tilted her head, his teasing tongue exploring her mouth and giving her such bliss—

The kiss ended as soon as it had begun.

"I really shouldn't," Lawrence breathed in a jagged voice.

Julia looked up with lust-hazed eyes. "Shouldn't what?"

His eyes flashed. "Do what I want to you."

Oh, God, if only he... "Yes, you should."

Lawrence groaned, dipping his head to her shoulder, then tilting to kiss her neck, making Julia gasp with uncontrolled pleasure. "No, I shouldn't..."

Her eyelashes fluttered, and Julia gave herself to the pleasure, adored the way his hands lowered from her waist until they were cupping her buttocks. She knew now the ache between her legs, this growing heady warmth in her stomach needed him to—

"Julia? Julia, is all well?"

With a moan, Julia stepped from Lawrence's embrace. "Damn," she whispered.

Lawrence's grin was as regretful as she felt. "I rather like hearing you speak so coarsely."

It was all Julia could do to remain upright, and if Lawrence remained in the hallway much longer, she would be only a puddle. "You'll have to go."

He sighed heavily. "And not a moment too soon, I dare say," he said ruefully.

A few steps, the open and close of a door, and Lawrence was gone.

Julia leaned against the wall, heart beating frantically, legs shaking as she tried not to think about what could have come next.

CHAPTER THIRTEEN

March 4, 1810

L AWRENCE SIGHED HEAVILY as he threw down another letter. *Well, he'd been doing his best, hadn't he?* Stuck it out here when Society wondered in the gossip pages and tattle sheets where precisely the Duke of Penshaw was?

Subjected himself time and time again to being punched on the nose so hard, he saw stars?

Tried to live like...like this?

Lawrence looked around, disgruntled. It wasn't that bad, he supposed. At least, it could have been worse. The place was clean, even if it was small, and it was not as though he would be required to do much hosting.

He almost snorted at the thought. *Hosting! Here!*

Lawrence Madgwick didn't *host*. There wasn't anyone he wanted to host in the first place, unless one counted...

He swallowed, forcing down the thoughts of the woman he most certainly should not have kissed a few nights ago, or the time before that, and certainly not the time before that, which had started off all this nonsense.

"Shall we return to Rotten Row, or do you wish to kiss a little longer first?"

And in her mother's house, too! God, if he had been known to be a duke at the time and they had been discovered...

Well, they'd be marching up the aisle before anyone could say "responsibility to make good."

Lawrence watched the flickering candle on what could just about be described as a desk. He had been unable to afford the very best wax, on account of him losing the last three fights.

On account of Julia being in the crowd.

"You're losing your touch," Alan had said bad temperedly only yesterday. "And it's all because—"

"Because I am looking in the crowd for a murderer," Lawrence had supplied, guiltily suppressing his conscience.

It was almost true.

It should have been true.

The candle before him flickered and almost died. Lawrence rose, pulled open a drawer, took out the last candle, and carefully lit the wick before he allowed a little wax to drop onto a saucer. Then he delicately placed the candle upon the cooling wax, waited for it to solidify, then returned to his chair.

John Mortimer. That was the person who should be consuming his thoughts every moment of the day. Had done, for months.

Before Julia appeared in his life.

When was the last time he had truly looked out into the crowd and searched for that sneering smile? Days? Weeks? Oh, it couldn't be a month, could it?

"Damned fool," Lawrence muttered to himself, leaning back in his chair and wishing he had more beef than potato in the pie he'd bought for his dinner that evening.

What did it take, eh? A man had killed his own brother, his sister was alone and unprotected—goodness knew what sort of louts had been circling her, a duke's daughter—and he, Lawrence, had done almost nothing the last few weeks to seek out the blaggard.

Lawrence's jaw tightened. He needed to focus. He needed to forget Miss Julia Dryden, a woman he certainly could not have—not until this business was over.

And surely this pit of anger in his stomach would never cease until Mortimer was brought to justice. Until he saw him in chains. Until—

"Hello?"

Lawrence blinked. A trick of his hearing, surely. *There was no possibility he could have heard…*

Ears pricked, he leaned forward and waited, head cocked like a dog. The walls were thin here; his landlady had tried to warn him about it when he had taken the rooms. It had not bothered him then.

The staircase went right along the side of this room—the room that was everything save bedchamber. And he had been certain…

Lawrence hesitated. Certain, yes, but there was no repeat of the mysterious voice. Perhaps he had dreamt it. Perhaps—

"Hello?"

It could not be Julia. *It was a common enough sound, a woman's voice,* Lawrence tried to tell himself. Absolutely no chance it was her. He had been thinking of her, that was why the voice had sounded familiar.

He snorted and leaned back in his chair. *Julia, here?* God, it was bad enough that *he* was here, let alone a young lady, still with her reputation to lose—

"Hello?" A knock on the door, genteel but insistent. "Lawrence, are you in there?"

Lawrence's mouth went dry. *What in God's name did she think she was—surely her brother was keeping a closer rein on her than this!*

Before he knew what he was doing, before he could stop himself or reason that if her being here was foolish, then opening the door—

He opened the door. "Jules."

Lawrence's voice sounded weak to his own ears, but it did not seem to matter to Julia. She beamed to see him as his heart rocketed in his chest.

Julia. She looked so out of place here, he almost laughed.

Wearing an elegant gown that did nothing but accentuate those delicious curves, Lawrence tried not to stare at the heavily rising chest. Evidently Julia had grown a little out of breadth, climbing all those stairs.

There could be no other reason that she was so breathless, could there?

"Lawrence," she said with a smile.

He continued to stare, hardly able to believe she was here. How had she found out where he—but then it would not have been hard, would it, to ask? Who would worry about giving such information? Who would suspect what she would do with it?

Lawrence's stomach twisted. He would have to discuss that with Alan, now he came to think about it. They couldn't have the whereabouts of the Duke of Penshaw so easily located, even if he was living under cover.

"May I..."

His heart skipped a beat. "What?"

Julia's smile broadened. "May I come in, or is it your custom to entertain guests on the landing?"

Guests? Lawrence had only welcomed, if one could call it welcomed, Alan to these pokey rooms. *Entertain?*

"Erm," he said, with no clue what he would say next. "I was not expecting—"

"Well, of course you weren't," said Julia smartly, taking a step closer and making it even harder to concentrate—if that was possible. "I thought I'd surprise you. That's all."

Lawrence nodded. What else could he say? She knew him as Lawrence Madgwick. She was hardly going to be shocked at the paltry conditions he was forced to live in, was she?

Stepping aside but not too far away that he could not breathe her in as she crossed his threshold, Lawrence watched Julia step into his room.

Her eyes widened with astonishment as he closed the door behind her.

That was the trouble with a room this small, wasn't it? It did not feel that bad when the door was open, when there was a sensation of greater space. But as soon as the door closed, when one was enclosed…

"Ah," said Julia helplessly. "How lovely."

Lawrence almost grinned. She was very well bred, indeed. It took someone with impeccable manners to find something pleasant to say about these rooms.

His gaze drifted across the small fire, lit with coke rather than coal—far cheaper. The bookcase he had ripped half apart for the wood. The plate, still dirty from his pie. The bottle of brandy that was half empty, no glasses visible.

What need he for glasses? Alan had called it medicinal, and Lawrence saw no point in arguing.

There were a few clean clothes scattered about the place, even more unclean ones, and his coat was hanging on a nail in the wall.

"Lovely," Julia repeated.

If only she had arrived at Penshaw Place, Lawrence found himself wishing. It was not like him to be snobbish, but really, this hardly reflected well on him.

Perhaps he should have attempted to keep it more tidy.

But the mansion, that was a far greater exploration of his wealth, his taste. The elegant Long Gallery, lined with ancestors in various fashions throughout the centuries. The sword his great-great, perhaps a few more, grandfather had wielded at the Battle of Bosworth. The lantern one of his relatives had used to aid Charles in his escape to the north.

Richness, splendor, pageantry.

Not a pair of moldering boots he really needed new laces for.

"Please, let me—"

"Oh no, I'll—"

Lawrence hesitated as Julia's chest brushed up against his and he halted, hardly able to breathe.

She should not be here. He should never have permitted her to enter, but now she had, he was swiftly becoming intoxicated by her presence. The beauty. The powerful charm she emanated, perhaps without even realizing.

The way she looked at him—

"I should have sent a note," Julia said with a smile, her eyes glittering. "But then of course, you may have said no."

He could hardly fault her there. "I probably would have done."

"There you are then."

"That doesn't mean you can just—"

"I suppose that is your chair," Julia said, stepping away from him.

Lawrence realized he had been holding his breath and hastily took another one to cease the fire in his lungs. She was pointing at the armchair. "Yes, it—"

"In that case, I will take this one."

Before he could say anything, Julia had picked up a few of the letters he had been reading before she had arrived and settled herself on the stool. "What's all this, then?"

"Nothing," Lawrence said hastily, snatching them from her hand and turning wildly to put them somewhere.

Dear God, if she were to spot a few words on those pages…would not the terms "murderer," "spy," and "duke" raise a few unfortunate questions?

"You surprise me."

Lawrence managed to ignore his racing heartbeat as he settled in the armchair, papers stuffed into the only book in the place, wishing he had thought to offer her the armchair.

As a gentleman should.

"I do?"

Julia flushed prettily at the statement. Lawrence cursed his own mouth for allowing himself to say such a thing.

The words a man might say to a woman, just as pretty as this, but in a church...

"Yes," said Julia, recovering herself sufficiently to continue the conversation. "I mean, I was under the impression that...well..."

Lawrence said nothing. It was not as though he knew what she was attempting to say, but it evidently was causing her more than a little embarrassment.

"Well, I thought you could not read," Julia managed to say, her cheeks a dark red now. "Forgive me, I just thought—most men of your class, of your background—"

He tried not to smile as she carried on attempting to explain herself. *Dear God, his cover must be excellent.* Did not think he could read? And here he was, fluent in Latin, Greek, French—

"—must think me silly."

"No," Lawrence said swiftly. *Nothing could be further from the truth.* "No, you would be correct in most cases. Remember, I had the mentorship of...of a duke."

The half-truth slipped so easily from his tongue, he almost winced.

Was this how liars were born? One found a lie that was convenient, easy to say, and was easily believed, and before you knew it...

"Well, I am glad you have something to entertain yourself when not in the boxing ring," said Julia cheerfully, as though she made it a habit to visit poor men in their rooms unaccompanied.

Lawrence laughed. *Well, he was not a duke, was he? He could say what he liked.* "Good God, Julia, you are a wild one!"

Though her cheeks were still pink, the mischievous grin that curled her lips was confident. "What, me?"

"You," Lawrence said heartily, wishing the chairs were closer. *If he could just reach forward...* "You are here alone, in the rooms of a man you hardly know—"

"Now that is not true," she countered immediately. "Yes, our acquaintance is perhaps not the oldest, but...Lawrence, there is no one in the world who knows me as well as you."

Her gaze met his, so intense it near took his breath away. *If he had fewer scruples...*

"I like your room."

He snorted. "You do not have to be polite."

"No! No, I do it's very..." Julia searched for an appropriate phrase. "Very charming."

Joy seared through Lawrence's chest. How did she manage it? Say so much and yet so little in just a few words?

She did something to him, this one, and if he was not careful, he was going to make a mistake, cross a line that had absolutely no going back.

"I like how...how Spartan you have kept it," Julia said, laughing herself now. "No, truly! It is easy to drown in fripperies and ribbons, trust me."

Lawrence could well believe it. He had seen his sister's last haber-dashery bill. "And do you?"

"Constantly."

"Well, you must not judge me by what you see," Lawrence found himself saying.

Now why had he said that?

True, it was not too revealing...unless, and the thought was a terrible one, unless Alan's suspicions were correct? Unless it was a little too convenient that this beauty had decided to attach herself to a man out of her class and beyond the realms of polite Society?

"No, I suppose not." Julia's eyes lingered on a sock. "But that leads me to ask a very important question."

Lawrence's stomach tensed. *An important question? What on earth could she possibly want to know about—*

"What," said Julia quietly, returning her gaze to him, "should I judge you on?"

Lawrence swallowed. The seemingly innocent gaze he knew so well was gone, replaced with...

Something new. Something different.

Still Julia, still those beautiful eyes, that proud mouth, that ability to look through him and make his insides become jelly because he could not stop looking at her.

But this was a more serious Julia. A Julia who wanted something, God knew what, and would not take no for an answer. She may not even leave the place until she got it.

A raw, hungry twist in his stomach was forced down—at least, as much as he could. No, she would not want that. She accepted his kisses, moaned at the way he touched her, but she was a lady!

A lady with a reputation. A lady who was under a deadline to marry.

Lawrence's heart thundered painfully as he gazed into that beautiful face. If only he had found John Mortimer already, he would be free, free to regain his place in Society, remove his cover, and put on once more the trappings of a duke.

Free to walk up to Mrs. Dryden and declare himself.

The very thought made red-hot flames spiral through his chest. But Lawrence couldn't do that. He couldn't even reveal himself to Julia, though he desperately wanted to.

He would not put her in danger.

And still she waited for his answer.

"What should I judge you on?"

"You should judge me," Lawrence said, his voice croaking, "on how I care about you."

Care about you? Care—what sort of paltry words were this?

Try as he might, Lawrence could not stride across the room, throw open the door, and remonstrate to her that it was most scandalous, risking her reputation in this way.

How could he when he wanted to open the opposite door? The door that led not to the landing and to relative safety, but to his bed...

"Care about me?" Julia repeated softly.

It was all Lawrence could do not to reach and trace those delicate lips as she spoke.

By God, he cared about her. Some marriages were made by appointment, some with just a few hours of acquaintance. It was rare that a man like him spent such time in the private company of a lady at all, let alone one who was an actual member of Society.

But he wasn't the Duke of Penshaw here, was he? Lawrence thought wildly. He was just Lawrence Madgwick. Lawrence, the boxer.

Lawrence, who Julia thought had no money, no title, no power… yet she was here.

"I care about you," Lawrence said, the words tumbling from his tongue. "Care so deeply, Julia, I—"

"Yes?" Julia said eagerly, leaning forward.

Lawrence swallowed. The gentle tilt of her body made the view of her breasts even more tantalizing than his imagination if that were possible.

God, he was only human!

"I…" He had to stop, he could not permit himself to become entangled—"Julia, I…"

Lawrence's words failed him. The room was closing in, the walls growing nearer, and all he could think of or look at was the woman before him.

Her eyes bright. Eager. But could she have any idea what was on his mind, any idea what he wanted?

Though Lawrence knew the danger he put both himself and her in by admitting even the faintest affection, he could not prevent it.

He had to tell Julia Dryden how he felt.

CHAPTER FOURTEEN

J ULIA TRIED HARD to keep her face neutral.

She failed.

She knew it, could feel it in the way her cheeks flushed, lips parted, chest rising and falling in a hasty rhythm, unable to take in what Lawrence had just said.

"I care about you. Care so deeply, Julia, I—"

And she had almost decided against coming! If it had not been for the kind man who recognized her from the many times she had attended the Almonry Den, she would have remained ignorant of where his rooms were.

It had taken a great deal of boldness to walk up these stairs. To knock on that door. To sit here calmly as though she did not have the most wanton thoughts rushing through her mind.

"I care about you. Care so deeply, Julia, I—"

And then he had said that.

"I...I hoped you did," Julia said softly.

What else could she say? She could hardly admit her own feelings.

Not that she knew what they were. *First*, she thought wildly, highly conscious of her fingers curling around the edge of her stool, *she would have to understand them herself.*

This heat, this need and longing to be near him—that was love, was it not?

Her admiration, the slight discomfort about his birth and background yet her ability to look past it. The way he made her feel like the center of a room, any room, whenever he was in it...

What was that, if not love?

"You shouldn't have come."

And in an instant, Julia deflated.

"I just meant," Lawrence said hastily, "that it was inadvisable for you to—"

"I know."

"And you may have been seen! Someone might have spotted you, your reputation—"

"I know," said Julia softly, a slow smile creeping across her mouth. *Did he not see?*

"—a woman such as yourself, vouchers for Almack's, the talk this could create—"

"I know," Julia said firmly.

"—and you, you...you're holding my hand, Jules."

Julia could not help but smile. *When was this rash, powerful, yet entirely clueless man going to understand?*

"I know I was bold to come here," she said quietly.

"Brazen, I call it."

"But why?" Julia said, jutting out her chin. "Ladies—women of your class do what they like. They tell men they have a fondness for them or that they like them, visit them in their rooms—"

"Julia."

It was not a warning, not quite. She saw in Lawrence a desperate desire to hear what she was going to say, yet a sense that he should not. That they should not.

Why, there was more gentleman in him than half the toffs she had the misfortune to meet at St. James's Court.

"You said you cared for me," Julia persisted. Her fingers were still entwined with his. "Well, I care for you."

Some strange shadow passed over Lawrence's face. "You should not say such things."

Rebellion rushed through her. She had been to the Almonry Den, not once, but several times. She had even made a bet once! She had spoken with a man far beyond her class. She had kissed him, not once but several times. Had felt the warmth of his breath on her neck.

Would do so again if she had her own way tonight.

And she loved him. She could not say as much. Julia was not so much a fool as all that, but still. He had to know, didn't he? Had to see it in her eyes?

"Lawrence, I..." Julia swallowed.

She had only been permitted out of the house at this hour—and out of that dreadful invitation with Miss Ashbrooke, the matchmaker to the *ton*—because she had promised Donald she would go and see Lawrence.

And break it off.

"Whatever it is, between you two," her brother had warned with a forefinger waggled in her direction, "it is to end. Tonight."

"Or what?" Julia had shot back as she had pulled on a pelisse.

"Or," Donald had said darkly, "I finish it for you."

Julia hesitated as she sat hand in hand with Lawrence, the words painful in her throat. But she had to say it. She had promised Donald she would at least say it.

"My family—my brother, I suppose I should say—does not want me to see you again."

There. It was said.

And on paper, Julia knew wretchedly, *it was the right thing to do.* Why, she was a lady! Of good name and relatively good dowry. She had a position to maintain, honor to preserve. She couldn't go around after boxers, or working-class men, or...

Lawrence. Julia's shoulders slumped as tension left them.

She was unable to fool herself. She would have to hope she was better at fooling Donald.

"Lawrence," she said.

There was disappointment in his face. Pain, a sort of heavy resignation.

"I understand," he said quietly.

"No, you don't," Julia said frantically. "It's just that—"

"Your family thinks I am of a…well. A different class to you."

Julia swallowed. It was so sordid, having it laid out like that so plainly, but that was the truth. She could hardly deny it.

Her gaze swept across the room. It was so unlike the pretty elegance of her own home. Harder still to consider this the sort of life she could choose.

But choosing Lawrence…that was something she could not so easily give up.

"Yes," she said softly. "A different class."

Was that a quirk of a smile across his face? "Well, I cannot say they're wrong."

"But don't you see, I don't care about—"

"You should," said Lawrence quickly. Somehow, he had let go of her fingers. "This is not the sort of life for a woman of your caliber, Jules, even if—I mean, not that I am asking you to…"

His voice trailed away as hope soared in Julia's chest. *Could he possibly mean…*

"They judge me for what I am," Lawrence said finally. "Your family. What they think I am."

And she knew so much better. She knew the passion in him, the power, yes, but also the softness. The care, the wit.

"It's my brother, really," Julia said awkwardly.

Lawrence laughed. "Donald."

"You cannot blame him, not entirely," she pointed out quietly. "He doesn't want his only sister marrying a boxer."

The words were out of her mouth before she could stop them.

Boiling heat flooded through her body, a blazing contrast with the temperature in the rooms. Julia dropped her head, her gaze settling in her lap.

What had she been thinking, saying such a thing? How on earth could she face him, anyone, after saying those words?

"He doesn't want his only sister marrying a boxer."

"Well? What do you think?"

Julia's head snapped up in shock. "I beg your—"

"I said, what do you think?" said Lawrence softly.

There was a strange sort of ringing in Julia's ears. *She must not lose her head*, she tried to tell herself quietly, as though she had any control over the matter.

It was not what it sounded like. It could not be.

Proposals were...well, roses, wine, music, getting down on one knee...

Julia's gaze roved over the strong mouth, bold eyes, and stubble on the cheeks of the man before her.

At least, that was what she had always thought. That they would appear in a shower of golden light, utterly expected because of course he would have spoken to her mother, and she would have spoken to her...

But perhaps proposals weren't all about the pomp and circumstance. Perhaps they weren't about riches and show. Perhaps it was about sitting on a damned uncomfortable stool, in a murky, undoubtedly damp room, with a man...a man you loved.

There was a teasing smile on Lawrence's face. "Well, what do you think?"

Julia swallowed. "If...oh, dash it all, Lawrence, I think you are teasing me!"

"I would never tease you," he said with a shake of his head. "At least, not about this."

Well, she had been bold enough to come here, hadn't she? What else had she hoped for?

"If...if you asked me to marry you, I might say yes."

"In that case," said Lawrence. "Will you marry me?"

"Not on your life."

"Julia Dryden—"

He was unable to speak any further. At least, he could have attempted it, but Julia had rather thoughtlessly made it difficult by falling into his arms and kissing him, none too gently, on the lips.

If she had been concerned about her reception, she should not have been. Lawrence pulled her immediately into his embrace, returning her passion with a kiss just as fervent.

This was it. This was everything. He was everything.

Lawrence rose to his feet, and Julia almost stumbled to the floor. "You mean it?"

"Yes."

"You'll really marry me?" he pressed. "With nothing for me to offer you?"

Julia stared in amazement. "Are you not worth anything?"

Lawrence did not reply in words. Instead, he took her head and pulled her the three or so steps it took to reach the only other door in the room. He opened it.

She gasped. He did not need to speak for her to understand what he was suggesting. Visible in the gloom was nothing in that room save…

"I love you, Julia," Lawrence said quietly from just behind her, his hand still entwined in hers. "I want to make you mine, more than— more than anything. More than Society, reputations, honor, all that nonsense. The question is, will you let me?"

She needed no further invitation.

Launching herself toward him and almost crying out at the relief of being once again in his arms, Julia kissed Lawrence heartily, parting her lips so her tongue could immediately meet his own.

It was like…coming home. Like finding one's place in the world. Her skin was tingling with anticipation, with the knowledge that only when Lawrence touched her was she complete.

It appeared he was just as eager to hold her, touch her, be with her. Lawrence's hands immediately cupped her buttocks, drawing her close. Julia moaned at the intensity of the sensation, the hardness now pushing into her stomach.

Oh, all she wanted was him.

"Julia," Lawrence moaned, raining kisses down her neck. "Julia…"

Julia arched her back, her body taking over—instinct knowing far more of what she wanted than her mind.

Her breath caught in her throat as his warm mouth closed around a nipple, scraping through her gown.

Oh, it had been a most excellent idea to leave her stays behind this morning…

"Lawrence," Julia gasped.

And he halted immediately.

She looked up with desire hazed eyes. "Why did you stop?"

"You said my name," came the reply from breathless lips. "I thought—well, that you wanted me to stop."

Julia stared, hardly able to believe what she was hearing. She had little experience of the lower classes of course, her mother had seen to that—but still, she was under the impression that men of that rank had appetites not easily sated.

In truth, she wanted to taste that appetite. The idea that he would stop merely because she had said his name…

"Lawrence," Julia said firmly—or as firmly as she could as she ached for his touch—"If I want you to stop, trust me, you'll know about it. Don't stop."

It appeared he needed little additional encouragement.

Julia gasped, her footing almost lost as Lawrence's ardor almost tipped her to the floor—*not the worst thing, of course,* she thought wildly.

The bed looked hardly wide enough to take the both of them.

"God, Julia," Lawrence moaned.

The desperation in his voice did something strange to her. Throwing all her aching desire in turmoil, she clung to him, raising her lips to his.

Because she was his.

"You'll really marry me? With nothing for me to offer you?"

Now, and forever. Mother's demands be damned.

"Lawrence," she moaned as his fingers half undid, half wrenched the ties of her gown.

The sensation of his fingertips brushing down her neck, her collarbone, her arms…

She had never before considered them particularly enticing areas of the body, but Lawrence was swiftly showing her that in the right hands, there was no part of her that could not be awakened.

"I fought this," Lawrence muttered as his hands pulled her gown to the floor, leaving her solely in her undershift. "Fought it so hard, you cannot know—"

"It appears then that you are a better fighter in the ring than in love," Julia teased, joy overwhelming her as tingles of pleasure shot through her. "Now kiss me."

With a growl, he ripped her undershift.

Julia gasped. She had expected to keep it on, though why she could not imagine. After all, if she wanted to delightful sight of Lawrence without clothing, she supposed she would have to do likewise.

Nothing could have prepared her, however, for the way his eyes widened at the sight of her breasts falling past the rent material, her hips now visible, and her secret place—

Julia moved to pull the undershift together. "I—"

"Don't hide yourself on my account," Lawrence said softly, capturing her fingers in his own and gently moving them apart. Moving apart the torn shift. "I want to see all of you, Jules. All of you."

Without taking her eyes from his, as though knowing her resolve would falter the moment the connection was broken, Julia allowed the undershift to fall.

Lawrence growled, pulling her into his arms. His forceful kiss claimed, did not ask.

And she gave it all to him. Why not? Why hold back what they were only to enjoy in a few short weeks anyway?

Had they not wanted this since...*she could not remember when*, Julia thought wildly as her fingers scrabbled to pull off his jacket, his waistcoat, his shirt, anything that kept them apart.

Since they had met?

"God, you're as eager for this as I am," Lawrence laughed under his breath as her fingers, after successfully ridding him of his waistcoat and shirt, tried to undo his breeches.

Julia grinned. "Why not? A lady seeks pleasure just as swiftly as a gentleman, I suppose."

"Though I," he whispered, pulling his boots off and breeches down, "am no gentleman."

She stared. Well, she knew the anatomy, of course, but reality was far different from theory.

There he stood, utterly naked, and there was...

"You're certainly a man," she breathed, her curious fingers reaching forward.

Lawrence twitched as her hand enclosed the tip of his manhood. "Jules..."

This was the moment, she knew, where they could just about retain some semblance of respectability and honor.

Well. Hers. A man like Lawrence hardly had it to begin with.

"Love me," Julia whispered, not letting go of Lawrence's manhood as she looked up into his eyes. "Love me, Lawrence."

"I already—"

"Love me as a man loves a woman."

Lawrence swept her up into his arms before she could say another word.

Another word was not necessary. Julia was laid gently on the bed, and before she could wonder where on earth he would find room for himself, he showed her.

Right between her thighs.

Julia moaned, the heady intimacy of Lawrence's chest pressed up against hers more than she could bear, and she accepted his kisses with wild abandon.

She had nothing to hold back now, no need to prevent herself from expressing the joy she felt.

And goodness, she felt joy, pleasure, something. A hot something, running through her body like a fire as Lawrence's hands touched her everywhere.

"I love you," he breathed against her neck. "God, I love you, Jules..."

"I love you," Julia whimpered, adoring the way his hips felt nestled between hers, the ache in her building. "Oh, Lawrence...Lawrence!"

He had entered her. She opened her eyes wide, almost astonished it had happened so quickly.

He mistook her expression. "I have put on a French letter, there will be no child until after we are married, when we can—"

Julia moaned as she arched her back, drawing him deeper in. "More."

There was silence for a moment. She opened her eyes and saw Lawrence gazing at her as though he had never seen her before.

"M-More?"

"Lawrence Madgwick," Julia said breathily, trying not to laugh. "If you do not see to my pleasure, I will have to take matters into my own hands."

He groaned at her words, dipping his head to take another kiss before murmuring, "I had always thought Society ladies so refined, so restrained—"

"Not this one," she said with a laugh, running her eager fingers over his muscular shoulders, reveling in his strength. "Now love me, Lawrence. Love me. Don't fight this anymore—I want this. I want you."

Lawrence crushed his lips against hers and began a rhythm with his hips that seeped pleasure into her very core, every inch of her being.

Julia could barely think, only feel, and she clung onto his shoulders as her hips rose to meet his, desperate to match his rhythm.

"Jules," Lawrence moaned.

She saw his adoration of her and knew that this may be the first time, their first time, but it would certainly not be the last. Her rough and ready boxer would be loving her like this for the rest of her life.

And then she lost all ability to talk. His hand on her hip, tilting her upward, increased the heady pleasure roaring through her, and Julia could do nothing but cry out as the ecstasy grew closer and closer, until—

"Lawrence!"

Her cry was one of abandon, of giving herself over entirely to the new pleasure and understanding they had now found.

Lawrence thrust heavily into her. "Jules!"

When he fell into her arms panting, Julia clutched him to her as though they were to be wrenched apart.

She would never give him up. Never.

Nothing could come between them now.

CHAPTER FIFTEEN

March 5, 1810

LAWRENCE GROANED AS he turned over onto his back, his eyes blearily opening to gaze up at the ceiling. There was still the same crack in it, the same horrible damp patch in one corner that he really was going to have to mention to his landlady.

He swallowed. His mouth was dry—but there was still a smile on his lips. *Why in God's name—*

Then it all came rushing back to him. The laughter. The pleasure. The feel of Julia curling into him, her soft skin warm and—

Lawrence's eyes snapped open.

"Now love me, Lawrence. Love me. Don't fight this anymore—I want this. I want you."

Well, no one could blame him. What man could manage to keep his hands from such a woman? And though she had not precisely offered herself to him...

"Lawrence Madgwick. If you do not see to my pleasure, I will have to take matters into my own hands."

A wry grin crept across Lawrence's face. Not exactly. But it was not as though he'd needed much persuasion. Not when faced with the beauty and elegance of a woman he had been in love with for some time.

Not that he had been able to admit it to himself.

But that didn't matter—at least, no longer. *Because,* Lawrence reminded himself, *you have made an agreement with a woman under false pretenses...*

"You'll really marry me? With nothing for me to offer you?"

"Are you not worth anything?"

A hint of guilt marred the joy soaring through his heart.

He had been in earnest when he had offered marriage, and it was not his fault if Julia did not know precisely what she had agreed to.

In a way, he tried to reason with himself, *she was to be applauded.* Julia was under the impression she had promised herself, after all, to a boxer with no prospects.

A poor decision for any woman, let alone a lady of the *ton.*

When he could tell her all... when Miss Julia Dryden would discover she was about to become the Duchess of Penshaw...

Lawrence grinned as he pulled himself up in bed, leaning against his pillow and the headboard, trying to clear his head.

It was difficult to imagine Julia's response to such a revelation, and in truth, he hoped to goodness he would be able to do so soon. It could not continue, this secrecy, this lying, this hiding in plain sight in the hope of discovering a criminal.

The sooner he could find John Mortimer, the sooner he could reveal all to Julia. Then it would not merely be a romance between them, but a full-blown love affair.

Not that, he thought with a snort, *they had held back much last night.*

It was almost like a dream, what they had shared together. Lawrence closed his eyes, images flashing before his mind of kisses trailing down shoulders, the little gasps of pleasure they tried to keep quiet, the way Julia squirmed in delight under his touch.

Lawrence opened his eyes. The squalid little bedchamber appeared once more around him.

There had been moments, last night, when he had almost been able to believe he was back in Penshaw. *That was the power of a good woman*, he thought ruefully.

Besides, it was impossible to consider the entire thing a dream, not when he could see a note on the floor by the door, in what appeared to be a delicate woman's script.

Lawrence half lunged, half fell out of bed, such was his eagerness to see what she had written.

Words of adoration? Perhaps a promise, and here he had to swallow in an attempt to keep his body from stiffening, to return tonight?

Oh God, if this started to become a daily habit...

As it was, the note was far shorter than he had hoped. Lawrence's heart fluttered as he sat on the end of his bed and scanned the few lines.

Well, I was certain you'd know how to please, and I judged right. J

Lawrence read the scant words again, hungry for any connection to the woman who had so entirely upended his plans to lay low under cover while fighting at the Almonry Den.

Well, I was certain you'd know how to please, and I judged right. J

His fingers traced over the initial at the end of her note. Julia. Was such a woman ever seen?

A clock struck somewhere down the street, and Lawrence carefully counted the bells before groaning loudly. *Ten o'clock. Blast. He was already late.*

It took a full twenty minutes or so, judging by the chimes of the quarter hours, to scrape a comb through his hair, make an attempt at a shave—he still wasn't very good at that—and dress himself in a sufficiently presentable manner.

So when Lawrence stumbled into the Almonry Den at half-past the hour, he was only—

"Thirty minutes late!" Alan roared with a scowl. "And don't tell me you were attending to your toilette, you look like you've been dragged through a hedge backward."

Lawrence chuckled, shaking his head as he clapped a hand on the older man's back. Nothing could dull his spirits today. "And it's wonderful to see you, too, you old dog."

Alan glared, then broke into a ruddy smile. "It's a good thing you're a better man than I, Penshaw," he muttered. "For else I would give you such a hiding—"

Lawrence knew it was coming. He dodged the thundering punch that would have made contact with his shoulder, ducking out and snorting with laughter as the older man almost tumbled to his feet with the follow through.

"Why don't you let me worry about the fighting, Alan," he said with a grin, looking around to see who else was practicing that morning. "I see there are few about so early. They aren't forced out of bed at this ungodly hour."

Alan snorted.

Lawrence ignored him. "So, what are we practicing today?"

This was the trouble with living undercover, he thought darkly, though ensuring to keep a smile on his face as he and Alan discussed footwork in loud voices.

It required a hefty commitment of time and manners, ensuring everyone around you was certain they knew who—and what—you were. Why, this time would be so much better spent if he could simply return to his digs and catch up on the sleep he had lost out while edging Julia to—

"I said, are you listening?"

Lawrence blinked. Alan was snapping his fingers before his eyes. Had been, it appeared, for quite some time.

He smiled weakly. "Yes?"

Alan raised a heavy eyebrow. "Oh, really? What have I been saying?"

Lawrence narrowed his eyes, willing his mind to creak into gear. It had been so much easier when he was younger. Chatting away under his breath with the other boys at school while keeping an eye out for the master, hoping he'd be able to answer any questions, even if he had not technically been paying attention…

"Footwork," Lawrence said, the vague memory slotting into place. "You are concerned my left foot is weaker than my right, you recommend a swifter balance change when retreating from an attack."

It was impossible not to feel a certain pride in the astonishment on the man's face. *Well, he was right, wasn't he?*

But it was not astonished that Alan's expression remained. When he leaned forward, a hand on Lawrence's shoulder, he looked serious. Far too serious, in Lawrence's mind.

What could possibly be wrong? He was engaged to be married to Miss Julia Dryden, the most beautiful woman in the—

"You're forgetting why we're here, boy," said Alan darkly under his breath, his eyes fixed on Lawrence's. "You came here because of your brother. Your brother and that blaggard. Are you…well, forgive me for saying so, but are you getting a little comfortable? Living like this?"

Lawrence's smile vanished.

"Because there are people relying on you, Lawrence," Alan continued, his voice low but every word weighty. "People will die if we do not succeed. The safety of this country is no jest, and I wish you could consider it with more care."

Lawrence stared into his eyes, guilt burning his lungs, every breath increasing it.

He could not deny it. Every word was true. It was just unfortunate it had to be said.

He was a Penshaw. A duke. He knew the responsibility he had to his people, his family, his nation. Was it really only a pretty face that was required to make him forget—

"There he is! Lawrence!"

Lawrence's stomach turned over in a most complicated somersault.

There she was. *Julia.* Standing there, right in the doorway of the Almonry Den, waving happily as though she were naught but a milkmaid, and their engagement had already been announced...

Another, slightly painful this time churn of his stomach rumbled through Lawrence's body as he saw who Julia was standing with.

Ah.

"Look, Donald, there he is!" Julia said clearly from several yards away, tugging her brother's arm. "I'm just going to say hello to..."

Lawrence glanced at Alan, fear now rushing through him. "I haven't told—"

"I know you didn't," said Alan quietly as both Julia and Donald started toward them. "But do you really think you can tell her why you're here, the cover you are living under, the danger we are in? Do you want her mixed up in this? For you to become distracted?"

Lawrence swallowed hard, his heart pounding.

Damn. Damn and blast.

But the man was right. Julia's face was beaming as she and her brother approached, all innocence—*well, not entirely innocence,* Lawrence reminded himself. She still believed he was nothing more than a poor man from the north looking to make a better life in the south.

And in a way, it was true. He had never been happy up there in the gloom of that big house, the heavy weight of his familial expectations weighing on his shoulders.

But there was so much more to him than Julia could possibly know...

"Hullo, Lawrence," said Julia slightly breathlessly as she and her brother stopped up before himself and Alan. "And how are you this fine morning? Did you have a good night's rest before your match today?"

Lawrence flushed to hear her say such things—*and right before her brother, too!*

It did not help that she grinned most mischievously as she spoke, a sparkle in her eyes telling him she knew precisely what she was doing!

The little minx!

How inconvenient that it made his heart beat faster, his shoulders stiffen…

And that was not the only thing that was stiffening.

"The boy slept well, I am sure," Alan said into the silence, evidently because Lawrence had not managed to unclench his jaw. "I am surprised to see you here again, Miss."

Lawrence shot a glance at Alan, but it was too late, the words were said. It was easy to ignore the rules of Society when Julia was sitting beside you, her hip nudging against his own.

Lawrence's jaw tightened. But to have her appear today, shout his name across a room, wave, drag her brother over…

The thought of her brother shifted his gaze, and Lawrence was unsurprised to see that Donald Dryden was just as unimpressed with the situation as he was. There was a coldness in his eyes that told Lawrence in no uncertain terms that this state of affairs could not continue.

"My family—my brother, I suppose I should say—does not want me to see you again."

Lawrence repressed a smile. *Yes, the man was right.*

Soon, he would be revealed as the Duke of Penshaw. Perhaps then the Drydens would be singing a different tune…

"—don't you think, Lawrence? Lawrence?"

"It appears to me the boxer has a little more on his mind than mere chatter, Julia," said Donald smoothly, cutting across his sister's speech. "Why doesn't Mr.…."

Lawrence glanced at Alan, who bowed his head.

"Alan—"

"Alan here will show you the ring, Jules," Donald said, waving a hand at the roped ring in which Lawrence would be within a few hours, hoping not to bleed too much. "I'll join you shortly."

Well, this was a turn up for the books, thought Lawrence. The man wanted to speak to him, did he? There could be no other reason, after all, for him pushing his sister away.

Julia gave her brother a strange look, one Lawrence would have surely imitated if he was not concentrating on keeping his face as impassive as impossible.

Damn. Damn and blast it all to hell. Did he know? Was it possible Julia had told...

Lawrence glanced at Julia's wide eyes and saw the answer there. No, she would never tell her brother what they had shared last night. If he was any judge, she would tell no one.

He gave her a brief nod encouragingly, and she beamed, unable to hide her affection.

Before Alan clearly knew what was happening, Lawrence saw with a laugh, Julia had slipped her hand into his arm and started promenading him toward the boxing ring.

"Now tell me, Mr. Oakley, I have heard tell..."

Lawrence watched them go, tried not to admire the shape of Julia walking away, and failed. That elegant sway making the fabric of her gown just hint at the curve of her bottom. Why, a woman like that could—

"Mr. Madgwick," said Donald quietly. "A word."

Lawrence almost sighed aloud, but he managed to restrain himself. *Well, if he had been in the man's place, he would probably have done something similar.*

When he lived as the Duke of Penshaw, if he'd caught a man being so free with his sister as he was with Julia, the man would be walking with a limp. If he was walking at all.

Throwing back his shoulders and ensuring his feet were on a level footing—just in case—Lawrence waited for the man to speak.

After all, it was only proper that Julia's brother have his chance to ascertain that all was appropriate between them. Even if it wasn't. Then he could reassure Donald—*Mr. Dryden, he should remember to be civil*—that his intentions were honorable, and they could all—

"Look, I have no wish to be rude, you understand me?" Donald brought out a cigar case nonchalantly from his waistcoat pocket. He drew out a cigar. The case was placed back into his pocket. "I am sure you understand."

Lawrence's jaw tightened. *Why, the blaggard did not even offer him a—*

"I am sure you would do the same in my position," said Julia's brother, lighting his cigar and taking a long drag. "It's a pain, actually, having to talk to you about this at all, but I tried to speak to her about this yesterday, and she utterly refused to break with you. You know Julia. Absolutely no concern for the look of the thing."

Lawrence smiled tightly. "Yes."

"And I am sure there is nothing wrong with you, per se. Probably a decent chap, if I got to know you. If you were ever at the Magnolia," said Donald airily, naming the club in London for those of middling income and even lower social status. "But of course, we haven't. Don't run in the same…circles. Do we?"

His eyes flickered to the boxing ring behind Lawrence, who swallowed as he turned back to Donald Dryden. The younger man was smiling affably.

"Let's be frank," said Donald, as though he had not been eminently obvious already. "You and Julia…well. You're not of her class, are you, boy? You're not good enough for her. Not good enough for most ladies, I would think, which is why you're here. But the more you spend time with her, the more you hurt her chances of meeting a real man. A gentleman."

It was all Lawrence could do to prevent a rather inappropriate speech from pouring from his lips.

A real—God's teeth, if the blaggard had any idea who he was talking to!

But he didn't, did he? Though a rising hot temper threatened to undo everything he and Alan had worked for, Lawrence managed to control it before it overflowed.

Because Donald Dryden did not see the Duke of Penshaw, one of the richest men in England, standing before him. He only saw a poor boxer with nothing to recommend him.

It was a strange situation, Lawrence knew, and one day he would make Donald pay for this.

In embarrassment only, he tried to tell himself. He would have no harm come to his future bride's brother.

"We had you for dinner, and all that, and Mother didn't exactly take against you," Donald was saying. "Very good at aping the gentleman, aren't you? But really, that is worrying within itself. You keep to your class, I say, and we'll keep to ours."

Lawrence allowed a crack of a smile across his face. "What you're saying is that you would like me to keep to my class, the rank in which I was born?"

Julia's brother snorted. Cigar smoke billowed around him. "Rank? Dear man, if you want to call it that way. Honestly, how can you look at her and believe you belong together?"

For the second time in the conversation, Lawrence looked over his shoulder. Julia was speaking animatedly to Alan, who appeared entirely charmed and was pointing at something in the boxing ring with great excitement.

Julia's head tilted, just for a moment, and her gaze caught Lawrence's. She smiled, her beauty lighting up. A jolt of desire and possessiveness roared through his chest.

She was his. He had taken her last night, and he would take her again, brother be damned. Not that he could say as such yet, of course…

"Now, I am asking you." Donald spoke quietly, and Lawrence turned back to him, discovering rather to his surprise that his hands had curled into fists by his side. "Man to man."

A flicker of irritation curled around Lawrence's heart. "What about as a gentleman?"

He should not have spoken. A smile crept over Donald's face that was most unpleasant to behold.

"A gentleman?" he repeated. "Why, I am a gentleman, yes. But you? You are not, and I would recommend you do not forget it. Do not forget what you are."

It was to Lawrence's credit—*at least, so he thought*—that he did not immediately reveal himself and throw off his cover which had been so poorly judged.

But of course, that was the point, wasn't it?

No one must know who he was.

"Thank you, Mr. Dryden," Lawrence said stiffly. "For your advice. I will not forget what I am."

CHAPTER SIXTEEN

March 9, 1810

"I PROMISE," JULIA said wearily, "I will be absolutely fine."

It was ridiculous. Why, she had lived in London all her life, knew the place like the back of her hand! There wasn't a street she did not know.

Well. All the respectable streets, Julia felt she had no choice but to correct herself silently. Of course there were parts of London she did not know—but that was beside the point!

In her mother's mind, however, it was clearly the point entirely.

"Anything could happen on these streets!" Mrs. Dryden said, waving a hand and almost immediately proving her point by whacking a gentleman in the ear as he attempted to pass them on the pavement. "Oh, I am sorry, my good man."

Julia rolled her eyes. *Why was her mother such a liability?* Was it the same with all mothers, or was she saddled with a particularly—

"And there is no need to roll your eyes at me, young lady!" her mother said smartly. "I saw that!"

Of course she did. Julia had known from a young age that her mother would almost always catch those irritated glances she shot her way, but she did not have to point it out. In public.

"Really, I do not know what has got into you recently," said her mother, tutting as she shifted a hat box in her encumbered hand. "You are…well. *Forward*, if you do not mind me saying so."

Julia knew her mother said so based on scant evidence, but the trouble was, she was hardly on solid ground to defend herself.

Forward. Yes, that was an accurate description of her behavior the last few months.

Far too forward, in Donald's opinion. But Julia could not regret her actions. How could she? Her boldness, her complete ignoring of the social rules and decorum at the Almonry Den had found her not just a companion, not just a man whose kisses threatened to stop her very heart one of these days…

But a husband.

A future husband. Julia glanced at her mother, fussing about her bonnet with her free hand, and bit her lip.

Deadline or no deadline, it was not the right time to inform her mother just what she had done—and agreed—with Lawrence Madgwick of Endell Street.

A smile crept across her face. Though she would have to tell her one day. She would have to plan the conversation to take place quietly in a dark room, where her mother's hysterics would not be too injurious to their reputation.

"I said, I will be absolutely fine," Julia repeated, seeing that her mother was assiduously ignoring her. "I know my way home, and I have no wish to traipse up and down with you searching for the perfect gloves—"

"I knew this would happen," her mother said dramatically, eyes wide. "Lady Romeril warned me of it, but I told her no, my daughter will never abandon me—"

"I am not abandoning you, Mama," Julia retorted, stepping to the side so a gaggle of ladies could rush past. "Really, if I knew you were going to take on so at the mere thought of me leaving your presence for half an hour, I wonder you are pushing me toward matrimony!"

It was the wrong thing to say.

Julia could see it, almost sense it, immediately. Matrimony. It was a topic she had carefully avoided over the last few days, after...

"You'll really marry me? With nothing for me to offer you?"

"Are you not worth anything?"

Her cheeks flushed at the mere remembrance of such words.

She was engaged. Engaged to be married—a secret engagement! Lawrence had not needed to request her secrecy; it was an unspoken understanding between them.

How could she reveal to her family that she had promised herself not to a gentleman, nor to a wealthy man, nor even—heaven forbid—to a titled man. But a boxer...

"Matrimony is different," her mother was saying imperiously. "Though I am glad you have finally brought up the topic. I am eager to discuss—"

"No, Mama," Julia said heartily.

Just a few more days, then she would have the courage—nay, the conviction—to tell her family.

And not before.

Her mother glared. "Well, you cannot say I do not push sufficient gentlemen in your direction, it is not my fault if you—"

"And on that note, I will take my leave of you and return home," Julia said swiftly, recognizing the beginning of one of her mother's monologues. "I will see you later, Mama. Good afternoon."

Bobbing a swift curtsey before her mother could say a word—an impressive feat, one which Julia had perfected over the years—she turned and started striding down the pavement, her skirts flapping in the early spring wind.

"Julia Dryden, you come back..."

Every step away from her mother lightened her heart. It would not be long, she was certain, and she and Lawrence could announce their love to their world. Their affection could not be contained forever, could it?

Julia hugged herself as the wind got up, memories tingling across her body of the lovemaking they had shared just days ago.

It was a shame that they had not found any additional time together. Parts of her ached for his touch, being away from him only increasing the longing.

They should discuss it soon. *Perhaps over a pie*, Julia thought happily, *or while watching a boxing match.* He had opened her eyes to such a world. How could she walk away from it? And thinking of walking…

Julia hesitated at the mouth of an alleyway. She did know London well, even if she had not walked down every street, and if she was not mistaken this would lead directly to Endell Street. Where Lawrence's lodgings were.

Why, she may even be fortunate enough to find him there.

She shivered, anticipation tightening her chest. She was not expected home for a few hours, if her mother's typical shopping trips were anything to go by. That would mean an hour or so alone with Lawrence.

She did not even have to think. Her footsteps took her forward into the dull gloom of the alley.

It did not take long for Julia to regret her decision.

In her mind, alleys in London were like veins, connecting the larger streets together. A hop, skip, and a jump, and she would be there.

She had not expected it to be such a long alley, nor so dark. There were a few women there, eager and expectant as she approached then disappointed as she appeared through the gloom.

"Penny, miss?"

Julia jumped, startled by the sudden appearance of a small child. What she had assumed was a heap of rags was a boy—or girl, it was hard to tell under the grime.

"I-I'm sorry," she stammered, quickening her pace. "I really mustn't—Lawrence!"

Julia's breath was knocked from her lungs as she turned a corner in the alley and came across the most horrendous scene. She could never have imagined such a sight.

She blinked, the darkness blinding—but no. She saw true.

There stood Lawrence, tall, shoulders broad, hands clenched into fists that were covered in blood—and for a heart-stopping moment, she thought he was injured.

But from the scene before her, it was likely someone else's. More specifically, the man who was lying on the ground at Lawrence's feet, his hands up around his face trying to protect himself, crying out for mercy.

"No—please!"

Wham!

Julia gasped as Lawrence's fist smacked hard into the man's stomach. The stranger groaned, coughing up blood, and Lawrence pulled back his hand to inflict even more damage.

"Please, sir, what did I ever—"

"Lawrence!" Julia cried.

She could not help it—it was a scene of such violence, such horror, that his name was dragged from her lips.

Seeing Lawrence punch a man was not unusual; how many times had she seen such a thing at the Almonry Den?

Countless. *Why,* Julia thought wildly as Lawrence hesitated, his left hand grabbing the man so that he could not escape, she had even cheered him on.

Why was it that the same actions in a different location felt so wrong, so horrendous? How was it possible to encourage violence in the Almonry Den, yet abhor it here?

Lawrence blinked, rage in his eyes seemingly dimming his view. "J-Jules?"

Julia took a step backward, her foot slipping. She almost stumbled into the wall behind her, her fingers clutching at it as though it could support not just her body but her mind which was reeling.

The man tried to pull away, but Lawrence was stronger.

"Lawrence, what are you—"

The man groaned. Lawrence had hit him hard about the head. A terrible crunch echoed along the alley, and the man fell to the ground, motionless.

Julia could hardly breathe, her chest frozen, heart racing, everything in her telling her to run, run away from this maniac!

But it was Lawrence. *How could she run from him?*

How could she stay?

"Jules, what in God's name are you doing here?" Lawrence spat a mouthful of what appeared to be blood before dragging the unconscious man toward her.

Julia whimpered in fear as he propped the man against the wall just beside her. What was happening? Where was the Lawrence she knew, the kind man, the man who fought in the ring for he had no other choice?

Was he just a thug?

"What am I—you are the one beating an innocent man to a pulp!"

Lawrence snorted, his eyes dark and his mood evidently grim. "Innocent man? Trust me, Jules, Mortimer got what was coming to him."

Julia's eyes flickered between the unstirring man—*he could be dead for all she knew!*—and the tall, handsome man before her.

How could she believe that? "What had he done to deserve such a beating?"

Was it her imagination, or would Lawrence not meet her eyes? "Never you mind."

"Never you—I beg your pardon!"

It had not been Julia's intention to sound imperious, but really! One could not simply go around metering out justice, if one could call it justice, merely because you had the biggest fists!

A strange pain was creeping through her lungs, and after a heartbeat's consideration, Julia realized it was fear.

She was afraid of Lawrence.

"I can't tell you about it now," he was saying, dragging a weary hand through his unruly hair. "But I did the right thing."

"The right..." Julia whispered, glancing at the motionless man. He was going to have a heavy bruise the next morning, that was clear. "You need to find a magistrate if you truly believe—"

"This is my business, Jules, and you would be best to be out of it—what do you think you're doing, walking down Grapes Alley!" Lawrence snapped. "Your brother isn't wrong, you know, you are too casual in your consideration of your own safety!"

Julia's jaw dropped. Now that, she could never have predicted. Her brother and Lawrence, agreeing with each other?

Where was his appreciation of her spirit? Where was his trust of her—why did he not explain why he had punched a man so brutally—

"I think you need to tell me what this is all about," Julia said stiffly, pointing at the unconscious man. "Why have you taken it upon yourself to be judge, jury, and if he does not see those cuts seen to, exe—"

"Damnit, Jules, I cannot tell you, so do not ask me!" Lawrence glared, his manner surly. "You don't understand!"

Julia blinked back tears. It was all too much: the shock of seeing Lawrence here, the fight, the blood, the vicious anger she had seen in his countenance...

He had enjoyed punching this man, she had seen that. He had never enjoyed violence before—at least, not that she had noticed.

Was this to be the beginning of their marriage? Complete honesty was what she had expected, yet she was supposed to accept random acts of violence, with no cause, no explanation?

"Of course I do not understand," she said quietly, grateful they were alone in the alley as they had this ridiculous argument. "How can I understand if you do not explain it to me?"

Lawrence made an irritated noise in the back of his throat and turned away, as though even looking at her was out of the question.

Julia swallowed. The panic in her stomach was growing now, climbing up her chest and into her throat. What did she know of this man? She had thought she knew him, thought she understood him. But there was evidently a part of Lawrence unknown to her. Was this the only part?

"I demand that you tell me."

"You don't get to make demands in this quarter," Lawrence said quietly, turning back to her, eyes haunted. "No one does. This is between me and—"

"Mortimer."

Lawrence swore quietly under his breath. "I should not have said—"

"Please, tell me," Julia said, reaching out her hand to splay it against his chest. She needed to be close to him. Perhaps their connection would return if she could just—

Lawrence pulled away. "Do not ask me of this, Jules, I beg you! You don't know what you're—"

"Then how can we get married?" Julia asked helplessly, hand falling to her side. "If you don't trust me?"

The words hung in the air, once said unable to be unsaid. Julia could hardly believe they had come from her mouth, but they had come from her heart.

It was unbelievable, this whole situation. She could almost laugh at the absurdity!

One moment, arguing with her mother about walking home, the next...

Coming across her betrothed violently attacking a man who appeared to have done no wrong but get caught in Lawrence's path.

"You are the one not trusting me," Lawrence said darkly. "You have to believe me, Jules, that when I tell you—"

"I cannot, I will not be told I am untrustworthy when I have not punched a man's lights out for no cause!" Julia hissed, pointing at the man.

Lawrence laughed. "Oh, there's cause."

She started, absolutely unable to take in what was going on. Cause? What possible cause could there be to be treated in such a way?

Julia had met her fair share of unpleasant gentlemen. The *ton* was full of them. Sometimes she'd had the misfortune to be placed by one at dinner, which was irritating to the extreme. A few times she had been forced to clear her throat loudly to prevent further insults.

Once, she had stepped very hard on Mr. Lister's foot. It appeared to be the only way to prevent him from leaning ever closer.

But never before had she encountered a soul that deserved such brutal treatment!

Julia glanced once more at the ashen-faced, blood-splattered man who had not regained consciousness.

If Lawrence had merely apprehended him, if the stranger had…oh, fixed a boxing match, perhaps. Stolen something. Then she could have understood. *Then perhaps*, Julia thought wretchedly, *she may have been impressed. Marveled at his restraint, at his sense of justice. But this?*

Julia turned her gaze back to Lawrence who blanched. "I trust you, Lawrence. At least, I trusted—I thought we had an understanding."

"We do—"

"We don't," she said simply. "Not if you can go around attacking men without cause. What is to stop this happening again? What if…"

The thought was so terrible, she could not even form words, but it did not appear necessary.

Lawrence stumbled back as though she had launched herself at him. His face was pale. "I would never, never lay a finger on you, Jules! How could you even think—"

"I never thought I would see you lay a finger on anyone outside a boxing ring!" Julia said desperately. *Why couldn't he see?* "Lawrence, if you can't tell me what this is all about, I-I can't marry you."

He stared, silent and unmoving.

"Well? Are you going to tell me?"

The time Julia waited, in the silence and gloom of the alley, could only have been about a minute.

Yet every second eked out as long as a century. She could feel her breathing, sense the rise and fall of her chest as she waited. She fixed her eyes on Lawrence's, begging him silently not to abandon everything they had, everything they wanted, merely for the sake of keeping a silly little secret.

Panic continued to rise in her chest. Lawrence looked wretched, but he looked no closer to opening his mouth than the man to her left was about to awake.

Eventually, Julia's shoulders slumped. She blinked back tears as everything she thought her life would be crashed down around her.

She had been a fool. Donald had been right.

"Fine," Julia said quietly. "Mr. Madgwick, please consider this engagement to be at an end."

"Jules—"

She slipped past him, feet rushing forward as though the very hounds of hell were snapping her ankles. Almost slipping as she turned a corner, Julia pressed on down the alley with only one thought on her mind—to get home as swiftly as possible.

"Jules! Julia, wait!"

But she had waited, Julia thought wretchedly as she dashed tears from her eyes, rushing past the women and into the safety of the main street. She had waited, given him a chance to tell her the truth, and he would not. He would not tell her.

And now all their chance of happiness was over.

CHAPTER SEVENTEEN

March 12, 1810

"WELL DONE, M'BOY," said Alan, shaking Lawrence's hand. "It's a triumph!"

A triumph. Well, thought Lawrence bitterly, *he supposed that on paper it was a triumph.*

A triumph which had been a long time coming. If only it had not happened right there, right then. Right in from of her.

"A most excellent result," said Mr. Snee formally, his mustache blustering as he continued. "I must say I was starting to have my doubts you know, but I should have trusted you. Trusted the process. That's what is important, after all. Trust."

Lawrence nodded blearily. It felt strange to be standing here in the justice's office, having handed over John Mortimer minutes before to the bailiffs' care. *He'd be in goal now*, Lawrence thought darkly, *while I am here, forced to drink bottom-of-the-shelf brandy with people who can think of nothing but celebrating.*

As if everything in the world was righted…

"Trust, indeed," Alan was saying formally, evidently delighted to be on speaking terms with a judge. "I always said to Lawrence, I can trust you to do this…"

"I trust you, Lawrence. At least, I trusted—I thought we had an under-

standing."

Lawrence's stomach curdled. Trust.

That was what Julia had thrown in his face. That he did not trust her.

Despite the many congratulations flying through the air, Lawrence could not help but feel empty. Yes, he had achieved what he had set out to do last year. Yes, his brother's killer and the traitor to the Crown was now behind bars, where he belonged.

God, he could now cast off the cover of Lawrence Madgwick and return to the world he knew. To better men. To better brandy, at the very least.

But how could he celebrate the end of his glorious connection with Julia? How could he walk away from this life knowing he would be leaving her behind within it?

"Mr. Madgwick, please consider this engagement to be at an end."

Oh, there was a chance that they would cross paths again, Lawrence thought wretchedly. In a formal dining room perhaps, over a tureen of soup.

Would she even recognize him? Would he recognize himself?

"—saying to His Grace here, enchanted to have him handed over," Alan was saying, clapping a hand on Lawrence's arm. "Yes, yes, marvelous."

Lawrence blinked. For a moment—a heart stopping moment—he had wondered who on earth "His Grace" was.

Who was he if he could not recall his birth? Had Lawrence Madgwick, boxer and general brute, become such a part of him that he was unable to leave him behind?

"Well, Your Grace, I am sure you are delighted to have avenged your brother," said Mr. Snee.

Lawrence nodded without saying anything.

What could he say? That he had expected to feel triumphant, glorious, powerful beyond the extreme, determined to shout to the world that he had been the one to bring down the blaggard?

It was all true, but it seemed to belong to a Lawrence, Duke of Penshaw, who no longer existed.

. All he felt was empty. A shell, as though his insides had been scooped out, placed on a plate, and handed to Julia…who had rejected them.

Mr. Snee settled happily in the large mahogany chair behind his desk. "Well, what will you do now, Mr. Alan?"

Lawrence blinked. Dear God, he had never thought to ask. Was Alan his surname, not his first name?

Alan spread his arms wide as he took in the expanse of leather and wood around the man's office. "Look for another way I can serve the Crown, of course, Mr. Snee. I am always at His Majesty's service."

The judge nodded sagely. "Excellent, excellent. And you, Your Grace?"

Lawrence looked at his hands. The nicks and bruising the devil Mortimer had exacted on him before he was subdued him were subsiding. Every day brought greater healing to the abrasions on his hands.

But what about his heart? What about his very soul?

A cough brought him to his senses. "What?"

"I said, Your Grace," repeated Mr. Snee with a raised eyebrow, "what will you do now? Now your commitment to serve as a duke in danger is at an end?"

Lawrence hesitated. "Go to the devil" did not appear to be a polite response. Certainly not one to make to a man who had the authority to clap him in irons if he thought the duke impertinent.

"Go to the Dulverton Club," he said.

Mr. Snee blinked. "I beg your pardon?"

"I am in need," Lawrence said, setting down his glass almost untouched, "of a good drink. I thank you, my lord," he continued, his voice growing stronger, more imperious with every word, "for your thanks and your hospitality, but I regret we must depart. Come, Alan."

181

He hated the way his voice so easily spat out orders. Almost as much as he hated how swiftly they were obeyed.

Alan was no servant of his; he was obedient to the Crown, not the name of Penshaw.

That did not seem to matter. With a nod of his head, Alan placed his own glass on the desk before him—Lawrence saw Mr. Snee wince at the immediate ring it started to make—and stepped toward the door.

"Any time I can be of service," Alan said with another bow. "Your servant, Mr. Snee."

"And yours, I am sure, Mr. Alan," said the judge in wonder. "And Your Grace, I wonder if—"

Lawrence had strode out of the room and closed the door behind him before he could hear a single platitude or request of the man.

Probably hoping for an invitation to Penshaw, he thought darkly. Well, he would need time alone there to get over this damned heartbreak before he permitted any visitors.

He almost tripped down the steps to the street. *Heartbreak? Now where on earth had that thought come from.*

"Well, that was damned rude," said Alan cheerfully, buttoning up his greatcoat. "The Dulverton Club, you say? I hope they have as good brandy as old Snee, I was really enjoying—"

"Far better, as you will soon discover," Lawrence interjected. "Come on."

They walked in silence, which was precisely how he liked it. When had conversation become so dull? When had the warmth gone out of the sun, color seeped from the world?

Lawrence gritted his teeth as they turned a corner. *Oh, he knew damned well.*

Admitting it to himself, however, was not something he was prepared to do.

The impressive columns of the Dulverton Club were a sight for sore eyes as they approached it, crossing the road just before an eager barouche rushed past them. Lawrence could almost feel the dread slipping from his shoulders.

At least here, he would be back where he belonged. Back, perhaps, where he should never have left.

"Ah," Alan said, clearing his throat awkwardly as they strode into the entrance way. "I've never been to—I did not realize it was quite—"

"The tradesmen's entrance," came a cool voice, "is around the back."

Lawrence fixed the footman on the desk with an imperious glare. He should have expected this. It was too much to expect that there would be a man here to recognize him.

Not that it would be easy. He was still dressed in the threadbare clothes Alan had sourced for him at the beginning of his assignment. His cover, Alan had said, must be impeccable.

Apparently it was so impeccable that the man at the welcome desk of the Dulverton Club did not even recognize the Duke of Penshaw.

"I think it best if we—"

"My dear man," said Lawrence sternly, cutting across Alan's hurried whisper. "Do you mean to tell me that you do not know who I am?"

It was strange. Returning to his old accent, the voice of his birth, came as quickly as breathing. Lawrence had wondered whether his rounder vowels would grow on him, but as it happened, he was able to slip into the tones of the Duke of Penshaw without a second thought.

Because, he tried to remind himself, *he was the Duke of Penshaw.*

Damn, this was getting difficult.

The footman looked aghast. "I—I did not think—Your Grace, is that you?"

Lawrence tried not to take this as an insult. In fairness to the man, his black eye was not entirely healed, and his clothes did stink something dreadful.

"It is I," he said calmly. "And I am, as you can see, in need of fresh clothes and a shave. Have a man made available, will you?"

It was a mark of the Dulverton Club's quality that it furnished him with bath, valet to shave him, and a set of clothes that almost fit within the hour. Within another five minutes, he and Alan—who had undergone a similar transformation and looked markedly uncomfortable—were sitting by a window in the Japan Room, proper brandy in hand.

Alan looked down suspiciously at his glass. "It doesn't smell at all right."

Lawrence smiled. "That's what it is supposed to smell like."

"Hmm." His companion did not look convinced. "If you say so."

It was a mark of how close they had become over the months that when Alan took a large swig of the liquid and choked, Lawrence did not laugh. He merely patted the older man on the back.

"You'll get used to it."

"I'm not sure I can afford to," spluttered Alan, placing the glass down on the small table beside him. It was going to leave a ring.

Lawrence let the warmth of the brandy revive him. But the liquor, fine as it was, was no miracle worker.

Well. This was his life now.

"You'll be in here often, I suppose."

Lawrence looked up at Alan, who had been impressively perceptive. "I suppose so."

"Balls and dinners and fine young ladies," said Alan with a grin. "All the comforts of life you've been missing."

Missing? Lawrence supposed he had. Missed that, that was.

He would certainly appreciate someone else darning his socks. He'd have to burn the remains of what he had. They were hardly fit for humans.

But what else had he missed? He had few friends; his brother had always been his closest companion, and his brother was gone.

Lawrence blinked back treacherous tears. He was not going to cry. Not here, not now, not at all. Dukes did not cry.

Besides, why would he want to return to a world that Julia was not in?

She was in it somewhere, he supposed. Lawrence had tried hard not to think about her mother's demand that she wed before the Season was over. Tried not to think of her attending balls, accepting the compliments of another man.

A man who, for some reason, had the same face as Mortimer.

Lawrence tried to unclench the hand which had unconsciously become a fist.

He had to harden his heart, push aside all thoughts of Julia, the life they could have had, the love they shared...

"You'll really marry me? With nothing for me to offer you?"

"Are you not worth anything?"

"You never said how you found him."

She should have trusted him, Lawrence thought bitterly as he took another sip of the delicious brandy. The golden amber burned his throat, reminding him he was still alive. But she had not. And he could not have a wife that did not trust him.

"Lawrence?"

"What?" Lawrence said, manners slipping back a little too late. "I beg your pardon?"

Alan was frowning. "I said, you never told me how you found him."

"Him?"

"Mortimer, you idiot, how much have you drunk?"

Lawrence would not have permitted such callous words from anyone save Alan. Of course, he had kept that part of the story to himself, far too interested in getting the blighter off their hands and into the nearest prison.

Which they had now achieved.

"It was...God, it was pure chance," Lawrence said, sighing heavily as his shoulders slumped. "I was taking a shortcut—you know, through Grapes Alley—"

Alan raised an eyebrow.

"I know, but I can take care of myself, and there he was. Just walking along it, bold as brass, not even attempting to hide his face," said Lawrence darkly.

It was a wonder. He almost hadn't recognized him, so lost in his thoughts had he been.

Lost in thoughts of Julia...

"My word," whistled Alan. "All that time in the ring and it was a damned alley. I suppose it was difficult to subdue him?"

Lawrence laughed bitterly.

"But you got the better of him," Alan said gleefully, sipping his drink. "This isn't so bad, y'know. Anyone with him? Anyone saw you?"

A mere shake of his head would have been enough, but Lawrence found himself saying, "No one bothered us—you know what it's like in those backstreets, no one wanted any trouble. And when Jules—"

"Julia?"

Too late, Lawrence saw his mistake.

Damnation and devilry, had he really permitted her name to slip from his lips?

It was no surprise, he thought as he shifted uncomfortably in the deep armchair. Her name had been so constantly on his thoughts since their argument, it was a wonder he had not mentioned her before.

"I trust you, Lawrence. At least, I trusted—I thought we had an understanding."

"Miss Dryden was there?" Alan said, all astonishment. "Blimey, you never mentioned—"

"It wasn't relevant," Lawrence snapped.

His brandy glass was empty. How had that happened?

"Not relevant?"

Lawrence sighed. It was all a mess, all of his own making. How had it come to this? How had such affection between them disappeared so swiftly?

Perhaps it was a godsend. If they could not traverse this, perhaps they were not well suited...

"Miss Dryden was there," Alan pressed. "My word. I admit, I am astonished she would be pleased to see you act in such a way, but then I suppose no man deserved a beating quite like Mortimer. How did you explain it to her?"

Lawrence's gaze drifted to the window. Wintery sunlight, no, spring sunlight he supposed, soared through it, illuminating the remaining liquor in Alan's glass.

He should lie. It would be easier that way, less painful. But it wasn't his way.

With every moment that he spent returned to his name, to his life, to himself, it became harder and harder to act with the impunity he had enjoyed as an anonymous man in the shadows.

He had to face what he had done.

"I didn't," Lawrence said heavily. "Our engagement—"

Alan choked on his brandy. "Engagement!"

"—is at an end," finished Lawrence.

They sat in silence as bitter regrets tore through his heart. It was not as though he could have done anything different. How could he have just explained, in the middle of an alley, what Mortimer had done?

Besides, it was a secret—a royal secret. The government would not have appreciated him gossiping about spies in the middle of an alley!

Lawrence shifted again. It was a poor excuse, but it was the only one he had.

"You," Alan said succinctly, "are an idiot."

Lawrence's head snapped up. "I beg your—"

"A complete fool," his companion reiterated, fixing him with a furious glare. "You maniac, you mean to tell me that you had Miss Julia Dryden committed to you, willing to marry you—a poor boxer with nothing to your name, for all she knew—and you let her get away?"

Lawrence's eyes were wide, trying to take in his friend's words. "Y-You were the one—you said...you always acted as though you thought I was too good for her!"

Alan snorted. A few heads further down the Japan Room turned at the uncouth sound. "Did I ever say that?"

Lawrence wracked his brains hastily, but the brandy had done its work, and it was becoming harder to focus. "No, but—"

"You idiot," said Alan companionably. "I thought she was too good for you! Too good a distraction, you nincompoop."

The room appeared to be spinning, but this, Lawrence knew, could not be blamed on the brandy. No, everything he had assumed about Alan's gruff approach to the beautiful lady who had walked into his life now had to be readjusted.

Too good for him?

"Look, it's as simple as this, and I am astonished I am having to explain it to a toff like you," Alan said heavily, leaning forward, as though he was about to explain a delicate piece of footwork.

Despite himself, Lawrence leaned forward, his heart skipping a beat. He shouldn't really indulge this desire to talk about Julia anymore—she was gone from his life—but he couldn't help it.

Just a few more minutes...

Alan fixed him with a beady eye. "Look. We had a job to do. She was a distraction, a major distraction, and if there's one thing you cannot have in boxing, it's a distraction."

Lawrence grunted his agreement. That was how men lost an eye.

"But you think I would have advised you away from her if we didn't have that brute to find?" Alan shook his head. "The moment you caught Mortimer you were free, free of the lies, the cover you had lived under...but in that moment, you chose your cover, not her."

It was hardly the most refined argument Lawrence had ever heard, but it did not need to be.

"The moment you caught Mortimer you were free, free of the lies, the cover you had lived under...but in that moment, you chose your cover, not her."

Oh, hell. He was right.

It had been the perfect time to explain—when his brother's killer was unconscious before him and he was free, free to be himself, to be the Duke of Penshaw.

But what had he done? Shouted, berated her for not trusting him when she did not know Mortimer from Adam, and then...

"Mr. Madgwick, please consider this engagement to be at an end."

Lawrence swallowed. He had just stood there, staring at the woman who made his whole body cry out, and said nothing.

"I am a fool," he croaked.

"Knew you'd come round to my way of thinking," said Alan smartly, leaning back in his chair. "Come on, Penshaw. There'll always be brigands, rogues, brutes. There'll always be blaggards, criminals to hunt down, whether you join me in it or not. But there won't," he said emphatically, waving a finger, "always be great women. Women like Miss Julia Dryden, for starters."

Lawrence dropped his head in his hands. "I am an idiot."

There was a snort of laughter from Alan. "That's what I've been saying!"

CHAPTER EIGHTEEN

March 13, 1810

J ULIA PULLED ON her second glove.

"I do not understand—"

"I know," she said curtly. "And that's precisely why I have to go."

"But, but, but..." her brother said helplessly. "I don't understand!"

Julia tried her best to keep her ire within. That's where she had to keep the anger, to remind her why she was storming out of the house, pelisse pulled roughly around her shoulders, no thought given to the undoubtedly freezing wind outside.

Because of what her brother had just said.

Well, let slip.

"But I didn't mean it like that," Donald said, coming round to stand before the front door in a clear attempt to prevent her from leaving. "I just meant—"

"Donald Dryden, you—you said something to him, didn't you?" Julia could not help the tone of accusation in her voice.

It was, after all, well merited. What had he just said to her over the breakfast table, cool as you like?

"I don't think we'll be bothered by that boxer anymore—and you can thank me for it later."

Donald's face was twisted in embarrassment. "Just a short conversation, a brief few lines, you understand, to make him see—"

"Make him see?" Julia repeated.

She could not recall being so angry, so utterly overwhelmed. Of course Lawrence had not felt able to confide in her, if he had been warned off by her absolute fool of a brother!

Evidently there was some danger involved—she should never have thought Lawrence could hurt someone without cause!—and thanks to her brother, she would now never know.

Because he was trying to protect her, wasn't he?

Not Donald, who stood there attempting to twist his tongue around an excuse that would be believable, thought Julia darkly. No, Lawrence. He had tried to protect her from something undoubtedly criminal.

And what had she done?

"Mr. Madgwick, please consider this engagement to be at an end."

Julia closed her eyes for a moment as though that would prevent the memory of how she had spoken to him.

Her eyes snapped open. It was no use. She had spoken unfairly to Lawrence. A few minutes was not enough time to consider, was it, if there was truly something important at stake. Particularly if her fool of a brother had demanded Lawrence leave her alone...

"—wanted to protect my sister, and I know you are older, and I am sure you will say you have no need of protection—"

And what did she really know about him? *About his past,* Julia corrected hastily in the privacy of her own mind. She felt certain she knew the Lawrence of now, of 1810, but what did she know of his past? What pains had brought him to London? What, perhaps had he been running from?

"—and really, all I asked of him was what any brother would—"

Julia bit her lip. It had all happened so quickly, that was the trouble. Perhaps if she'd had time to think...in that alley, dark and damp, everything had felt dangerous. She had demanded an explanation, but perhaps it was not her right to demand.

"—once you think about it, I am sure you will appreciate just why

I—"

"—ruined any chance of my happiness?" Julia interjected, eyebrow raised.

Her shoulders slumped as Donald gaped.

He had probably meant well, in his way. Julia knew brothers felt this sort of thing awfully, particularly when there was no father in the picture. Maybe if she had been in his place, she would have done something similar. Whatever it was.

"Let me get this straight," Julia said, raising a warning finger at her younger brother. Donald gazed at it nervously. "You do not like Lawrence, so you warned him off—"

"It's not that I don't like him," said Donald wretchedly. "It was just…well. He's not our sort, is he?"

Julia tried to keep calm. After all, it was the sort of thing she might have said a year ago. Before she met Lawrence. Before she discovered there was more in common between someone of her breeding and someone of his birth than she could ever have predicted.

"You said a few days ago that you were a common man, a working-class man, a man who earns his bread with his hands, did you not?"

"He is not our sort, no," Julia said stiffly. She saw Donald relax and barreled on regardless. "He is infinitely better."

Her brother's mouth fell open. "Julia!"

"He doesn't judge a person's merit based on what they look like or how they speak or whether they know the right fork to use!" Though now she came to think about it, he was rather well versed in the delicate art of cutlery… "Lawrence looks at a person for who they are, underneath all that!"

"I bet he does," came the unfortunate remark from her brother.

Julia glared, though her treacherous cheeks flushed at the same time. She was not about to admit to such things to her brother, of all people!

"You have potentially ruined my happiness, Donald," she said quietly, hand dropping to her side. "I know you meant well, but you really mustn't meddle in the affairs of others."

"Affairs?"

Ah. Julia probably shouldn't have used that particular word to describe...

Her brother's face now looked stricken. "Do you mean to tell me I've now got to go back and beg him to take you, fight the man to force him to marry—"

"You will do no such thing," Julia said firmly, cheeks still blazing. *The very thought!* "Just let me go to him, Donald. Get out of my way and pray you haven't ended a respectable marriage for me."

"Respectable marriage?"

Julia groaned. *Oh, it was getting worse and worse!*

Their mother swept into the hall. "Did I hear you have made a respectable—"

"Can't wait, very important engagement to attend to," Julia said breezily, shoving her brother none too gently to the side and pulling open the door.

She had to get out, escape the house before her mother—

"And what engagement is that?" Mrs. Dryden called after her.

Julia grinned mischievously as the spring wind caught at her hair. "My own!"

She had slammed the door and raced down the street before she could be called back.

Her brother had tried to warn off Lawrence. That much was clear. That had to be the explanation for his wooden conversation in the alley.

If Lawrence had been told to stay away from me, Julia thought wildly, *he had no choice but to stay silent.* Donald must have exacted some sort of promise!

The thought made her heart sing. It accounted for everything, and best of all, meant Lawrence still cared for her. They loved each other, didn't they? They wanted to be together.

And they still could be.

The streets of London were busy. Julia pushed past people, her pace slowing with every step as it became more and more difficult to advance. It was going to take her forever to get to Endell Street like this! Unless…

Julia glanced to her left and saw the dark opening to an alleyway.

Despite not knowing the route of this one in particular, it went off to the left. Even if it did not take her all the way to Endell Street, it had to get her closer than she was now. It was a risk, particularly after what had happened the last time she had traversed down an alley.

"Careful there, pianoforte coming through!"

Throwing up her hands, Julia acted on instinct. She slipped into the alleyway.

It was far colder here, but most importantly, it was almost empty. Julia hurried along, pulling her pelisse closer as she continued. The alley extended longer than she had expected, twisting and turning, until finally—

"Hullo, miss."

Julia came to a sudden halt. It was that or barrel directly into the broad chest of a leering man at least a head taller than her who had suddenly stepped out into her path.

Her breath caught in a throat for a moment, such was the surprise. How did a man stand so still and so dark in the shadows like that.

"H-Hello," she said breathlessly. "L-Let me pass, please."

She had not intended it to be a request. That, Julia swiftly saw, was her first mistake.

Her second mistake was not attempting to push past him. Instead she hesitated, and that gave his two friends time to step out of their own shadows.

One behind her. One to the side.

Julia swallowed. *Another person would surely be coming down this alleyway any moment,* she tried to tell herself, heart pounding painfully in her chest. It was all a misunderstanding anyway. She undoubtedly looked like an acquaintance of theirs, and as soon as that mistake was cleared up...

She glanced at the man to her side, saw the way he looked at her, eyes gleaming with a hunger that she had no interest in satisfying. Something painful twisted in her stomach.

"What is a young lady like yourself doing in a place like this?" leered the first man.

Julia turned back to him and wished immediately she had not. He already seemed to be taller, broader. More unpleasant.

"I am going to see my—my friend," she said, trying to keep her voice firm. "He's a boxer, very tall, you probably know him, Lawrence—"

"A boxer, eh?" The man's voice behind her was quite unlike the first. Softer, quieter. More dangerous. "I suppose he's taught you a thing or two, eh?"

The lecherous laughter crowded Julia's mind, but it brought to mind...

"Right, then you'll need to raise your hands up like—no, not like that..."

Horrendous as the men were, they were right. Lawrence had taught her something—not much, and if she had any other choice, she would not even consider attempting it.

But what choice did she have?

"Now, you stand like this. See? Feet like this? More apart."

Slowly, Julia shifted her feet so that she was standing in a better position, her mind desperately attempting to recall every piece of advice Lawrence had given her.

Oh, if he could see her now!

Panic rose in Julia's chest as the men started to laugh.

"Look at her, trying to act all brave," one said.

Julia flushed but knew she could wait no longer. It appeared no one else was going to walk down this alley—a clever decision on their part, she could not help but think wretchedly, if they knew who was within it.

That meant she had to act, now. Before something terrible happened.

If it had not happened already.

She lunged, punching out her fist in the way Lawrence had taught her. It had felt wonderful when the two of them had done it together, moving forward in the dappled light of the Almonry Den.

It felt awful now. Her fist connected with the chest of the tall man but made absolutely no difference. He merely laughed as she missed her balance and whirled helplessly to face another one of the men.

"A little fighter, we have here," one of them laughed darkly.

Julia pushed back her hair and tried not to think about what was going to happen next. If she had only offered them her reticule right at the beginning, perhaps she—

"That she is," said a voice she knew. "Far more impressive than you three, certainly."

"Lawrence," Julia breathed.

There he stood, just beyond them in the gloom, a dark and dangerous expression on his face as he glared at the miscreants.

Julia's shoulders sagged with relief, panic dissipating the moment she knew he was here.

"She's ours, you can have what's left after we—"

Lawrence moved so swiftly, Julia could not understand how he had done it. He lunged at the tall man, fists flying furiously, nimbly ducking under the slower punches that came at him, and within a moment, the biggest man was lying on the ground howling, blood pouring from his nose.

"You little—"

Lawrence did not wait for the second man to complete his sentence. He rushed him, pushing him into the wall of the alley. Julia raised a hand to her mouth as the man's head whacked against the brickwork. He slumped, unmoving.

She looked up, astonished at how eager she was to see the third man face Lawrence—but he had gone. The smallest, sniveling man had evidently decided facing the boxer was simply not worth it. His fleeing footsteps echoed down the alley.

"Julia?"

Julia blinked, hardly knowing what was about to happen next. "Lawrence?"

His hand was outstretched, his face grim. "Come on."

She did not think. Her fingers entwined with his, and Lawrence pulled her.

They rushed down the alley in the direction he had come, the direction of the Almonry Den, Julia was sure. After a mere minute, they were gasping for breath out on a street almost dazzlingly bright as respectably dressed people passed them with tuts on their lips.

"Really!"

"Can't even get out of the way!"

Julia put out a hand, attempting to reach the wall so she could keep her balance. What she ended up splaying her fingers against was just as strong but far warmer.

"Julia?"

She looked into the worried eyes of Lawrence Madgwick, and her heart soared.

He had saved her.

"Lawrence," she said weakly.

"Are you quite well?" His urgent question was accompanied by his flickering gaze. "Julia, did they hurt you?"

"No," Julia shook her head, then immediately desisted, the ground swaying before her. "No, they did not touch me."

She braced herself for the next comment, which she knew would come. At least, if her mother or brother were here, they would certainly have followed up with the obvious.

"What were you doing down there? How could you put yourself in danger? Why don't you take care to—"

But no such questions came. Lawrence crushed her into his arms, his embrace desperate as his fingers clung to her shoulders.

"I am so relieved you are safe."

Julia's hands wrapped around his thick muscular torso and only then, eyelashes fluttered shut, did she allow herself to truly relax.

She was safe. She was with Lawrence.

How long they stood there, she was not sure. Long enough for her frantic breathing to slow to match the steady rise and fall of his chest. Long enough to realize she wished to be nowhere else in the world but in his arms. Long enough to be an inconvenience, it seemed.

"Standing there, bold as brass, embracing!"

Julia slipped from his arms with flushed cheeks. "I suppose we should—"

"Yes," said Lawrence quickly. "Come on."

She blinked as he placed her hand on his arm and started walking them along the street. What she had been about to say was, "I suppose we should say goodbye."

After all, had she not broken with him? Would he not be angry with her, upset she had so summarily ended their engagement?

But there did not appear to be upset in Lawrence's eyes, at least not from what Julia could see as she shot glances at him as they walked. Only after a few minutes did she realize where they were going.

"The Dulverton Club—but Lawrence, we cannot—"

"No, not quite," said Lawrence with a wry smile that made joy prickle into her heart. "Not yet, anyway."

Not yet? Julia could not understand it, and she was even more confused when he instead strode past the Dulverton Club—a place Donald had once talked about attempting to join but had sheepishly returned home without saying a word—and up the steps of a grand house that appeared to occupy half the street.

"Lawrence, what are you—"

"I need to talk to you," said Lawrence, utterly ignoring the fact that they were striding into someone's house, and one far too impressive for the likes of them. "Come on."

"But—oh, my."

Julia stared as Lawrence shut the door behind them. It was hard not to.

The entrance hallway was absolutely magnificent. Marble adorned every surface, the floor, the walls, the ceiling. Elegant paintings hung on the walls, gold gilt frames glittering in the light of several candles in the chandelier above. Several doors led off the hall, each of them beautifully carved oak. A console table with a clock and several ornaments was the centerpiece just to the left of a sweeping staircase lined with red velvet carpet.

Julia swallowed. Whatever Lawrence thought he was doing, the owner of such a place would surely not take kindly to—

"I love you."

And all her concerns melted away. "You do?"

Lawrence nodded, his handsome face twisting in an awkward smile. "I may not have always shown it, but God, Jules, you are everything to me. Every moment since I met you has been an exercise in attempting to know you better."

Julia's heart leapt. "You have rather succeeded."

"Not enough," he said. "I should have known, in Grapes Alley, that your sense of justice would not cease unless you knew why I…"

His voice trailed away as guilt swept through Julia's chest. She should never have doubted him. It seemed so clear, away from that dark place, standing in this place of opulence.

"I should not have pushed you," she said gently. "I—"

"He killed my brother, you see."

Julia's jaw fell open.

Oh, dear God. It was worse than she could ever have imagined.

Lawrence nodded ruefully. "I couldn't tell you because…well, because Mortimer had done more than murder. He is being held now for treason, actually—"

Julia's mind struggled to keep up with these revelations, coming swift and fast. *Murder? Treason?!*

"—and so I did not know whether I could...well," said Lawrence, hands outstretched apologetically. "Spill state secrets. There it is. I am sorry."

"No—no, it is I who am sorry!" Julia blurted. "I should not have pushed you. I should have known there would be a reason..."

Oh, how could she have been so blind?

"I had hoped if I could explain this to you even in part, you would...well," Lawrence said awkwardly. "Still wish to marry me."

And the world made sense once again. Julia grinned, unable to restrain herself as she stepped forward and kissed Lawrence hard on the mouth.

It was becoming rapidly clear, as Lawrence's arms encircled her, his hands on her buttocks and heat blossoming between them as they each claimed pleasure after pleasure, that if they did not leave whoever's house this was soon, Lawrence was going to take her right here, right now, on this marble floor.

Julia pulled away, taking a step back to prevent herself from succumbing to such a temptation. "So you'll still marry me?"

"Try and stop me," Lawrence growled, hunger on his lips, though for some reason, he hesitated. "At least...there is just one problem."

"That you're likely to be arrested for breaking and entering?" she quipped with a grin.

Lawrence pushed his hair back with a wry grin. "Rather difficult to be arrested for kissing one's betrothed in one's own home."

It took a moment for the words to sink in. *In one's own home?*

Then Julia's mouth fell open as astonishment rocked her. "One's own...Lawrence. Do not tell me you own this place."

"Fine, I won't tell you," he said with a laugh. "But it's true."

"True?"

This was some sort of jest, surely, Julia thought wildly—but a strange sort of jest. If he owned a place like this…

"Lawrence," Julia said slowly. "You said once we were from very different classes—no, different ranks, you said. Ranks."

And as she looked at him, the easy way he stood there, the regal elegance of his features, the complete nonchalance of the man…

"You're rich," she breathed.

"Not quite."

"Oh."

"I'm fabulously rich," Lawrence said with a laugh. "And a duke, too, now I come to think about it."

Julia's legs started to quiver. "A duke?"

"I hope that won't be a problem," he said, seriously.

It was a good thing she was not too far from the stairs. Julia managed to drop onto the third step. She looked up at the man—*the gentleman,* she corrected herself with a thumping heart—who had secured her affections when she had believed him naught but a boxer.

A duke…

"I had thought you'd guessed," said Lawrence quietly, slipping down beside her on the stairs. "At your dinner."

Julia laughed dryly. "You would have thought so, but apparently not!"

Her mind was whirling, trying to take it all in. *A duke!* But then, he was so elegant in his speech, so refined. He knew about the oyster fork!

And all this time, he had been living in those horrid digs and punching men in the boxing ring?

"I was undercover," Lawrence said softly, as though able to read her thoughts. One of his arms slipped around her shoulders, while his other hand took one of hers. "I had to be, to catch the blaggard—sorry, the man who killed my brother."

"Undercover?" Julia repeated helplessly.

He nodded, his eyes serious now. "I did not want to deceive you, deception is not in my nature, but…oh, Jules. You loved me when you thought I had nothing, when I was nothing. Can you bear to marry me now, when I have so much to offer?"

There was a teasing look in his eyes, but Julia saw through the levity.

"It would be a great responsibility, I suppose," she said slowly. "Becoming a duchess."

Lawrence shrugged. "I suppose it will be. But there's always an alternative."

Julia breathed in deeply, but this did not aid her concentration. Not with Lawrence so close, the musk of his efforts in the alleyway invading her nose, obliterating all self-control. "There is?"

He leaned forward, slowly, his lips moving closer to hers. "We could always go undercover again…"

CHAPTER NINETEEN

March 25, 1810

"—AND I SAID to her, I said, my future son-in-law, the Duke of Penshaw—"

Lawrence heard Julia groan from the other end of the sofa and suppressed a hearty grin as Mrs. Dryden spoke with bright eyes opposite them.

Well, it was to be expected. He had always known, hadn't he, that when—*if*—he ever found a woman he liked enough to marry, there would be a flutter of excitement.

Not just in the family, but in Society. It was not every day that a duke decided to wed.

Still. He could not decide what was more amusing: the mother, the son, or the daughter's reactions.

"No hard feelings of course, old man, eh, eh?"

Lawrence looked up to see Donald standing awkwardly by the magnificent fireplace in the Penshaw townhouse drawing room. The younger man had that look on his face that told quite plainly, unless he received specific forgiveness, in the presence of his mother, said mother was liable to hold it over him for the rest of his life.

"You and Julia...well. You're not of her class, are you, boy? You're not good enough for her."

Much as he had disliked the tone the young man had used in their last conversation, Lawrence was not one to hold a grudge. Not when the welp had so clearly learned something.

"Not at all, old thing," Lawrence said pleasantly, seeing the relief soar through Donald's expression. "An easy mistake to make, when a man is working as a boxer at the Almonry."

Julia winced and only too late did Lawrence remember. *Oh, blast. They had agreed not to permit her mother to discover—*

"The Almonry? What is that?" said Mrs. Dryden eagerly. "I did not know there was another club in London—Donald, you shall have to ensure you have membership, if His Grace is also a member!"

Lawrence glanced at Julia as he stifled a chuckle. She was in absolute paroxysms of agony, he could see, but it was her own fault.

She was the one who wanted to keep the story of how they had met and fallen in love a secret. She was the one too afraid to own up to her mother where she had been spending so much time the last few months. If it were down to him…

Lawrence smiled at Julia and stretched out his hand. She took it eagerly.

Out of the corner of his eye, Lawrence could see that Mrs. Dryden had raised an astonished eyebrow at the obvious display of affection. He did not relinquish Julia's hand.

Nothing could make him do so now.

"I do not think I shall be frequenting the Almonry D-Club any longer, madam," Lawrence said smoothly, turning back to Mrs. Dryden, who had pinked with delight. "I think it not quite right for my tastes. Not any longer."

"Oh, well, your taste I am sure is impeccable, Your Grace, so I—*we* will be guided by you," Mrs. Dryden gushed. "After all, I knew it, did I not! The moment you dined with us, I knew, didn't I, Julia, that you were undoubtedly a man of great rank and fortune!"

Lawrence felt, rather than saw this time, Julia's wince. A small tightening of her grip on his hands, her pulse quickening.

Her mother was beaming, obviously delighted at having secured such a son-in-law, and on paper Lawrence could not blame her. It was an excellent coup.

Particularly as her daughter had accepted him with no idea of his title...

"As I said to Lady Romeril—you know Lady Romeril, I am sure, Your Grace—"

"I do not believe there is a soul in the world who does not know of Lady Romeril," Lawrence said gravely.

There was a muffled snort of laughter on his left.

"Precisely, such an elegant woman," Mrs. Dryden continued blithely. "As I said to her, you know, my future son-in-law, the Duke of Penshaw—"

"You did not say such a thing, Mama!" Donald groaned, settling in an armchair with a look of great distaste. "Do you not think it unseemly to be bandying about the name of—"

"Unseemly? You would think to dictate to me, young man, what is seemly?" His mother drew herself up. "Well! I am sure the Duke of Penshaw has never heard such a thing, a son criticizing his mother so! I do apologize, Your Grace."

Lawrence blinked. The apology seemed unnecessary. "Oh. Right. I, uh—"

"As I was saying, before I was so *rudely* interrupted," said Mrs. Dryden, glowering at her son, "when speaking to Lady Romeril of the future grand addition to our family—"

"This is absolutely intolerable," Julia hissed under her mother's monologue. "What on earth were you thinking, inviting them here?"

Lawrence had to laugh. In a way, she was right. So accustomed had they been to having time together alone, or at least, alone in a crowd at the Almonry Den where no one gave them a second glance, it was rather jarring to be forced back into company.

He had been away from polite Society for so long, he had forgotten its formalities.

But now they were engaged, and he was once more officially the Duke of Penshaw—*some of the grime*, Lawrence thought darkly, *would never come off*—everything was different.

If they wished to converse, they had to do so in company. If they wished to walk in a park, they were accompanied.

And if Julia was to do the unthinkable and actually spend time in the duke's home...

Why, her family must chaperone her.

"—suppose that makes me a dowager duchess—"

"Mama, you know it does not!"

Lawrence grinned at the outrage in Donald's voice. "At least your mother can be kept occupied by your brother."

"Yes, but for how long?" whispered Julia with a laugh. "This is becoming impossible—how long before we can wed?"

"Weeks," Lawrence said heavily. "Weeks too many."

Special license was of course the only solution, but even then, one had to wait during weeks of torment.

Lawrence tried not to think of the warm, delectable body of the woman seated beside him. Of the skin hidden just under a few layers. The taste of her, the way she writhed—

He shifted slightly in his seat. *Oh, blast.*

"What is—ah." Julia's eyes flickered down to his breeches as a smile crept across her face. "Most unfortunate."

Most unfortunate? Lawrence could have groaned with agony if they were not so unfortunately accompanied. *It was more than unfortunate; it was torture!* How was he supposed to suffer through one more night without her?

"—and wedding planning takes up so much time, it is a wonder I am getting anything else done," his future mother-in-law was wittering on. "Why, as I said to—"

"I am sorry that it is such a burden, Mrs. Dryden," Lawrence said seriously, interrupting her flow. "If you wish, we could reduce your stress by cancelling the wedding."

It was unfortunate that at that moment, Donald had been taking a sip of tea.

Brown liquid spurted across the room. Julia burst into hysterical laughter, Mrs. Dryden immediately started to berate her son, and Lawrence watched with general amusement at the whole scene.

"Disgusting boy, hardly able to take you—"

"So sorry, Lawrence—blast, I mean Your Grace, I did not mean to—"

"—all over His Grace's carpet!"

Julia's giggles shot joy right through Lawrence's chest as he started to laugh himself. Oh, it was going to be an adventure, being a part of this family. His own had been so refined, so distant—his brother someone to admire from afar, his sister someone to protect.

But perhaps that would change. Perhaps, now he had Julia and this warm and open example of a family, he could learn something new.

A new way to be happy.

"—must forgive him, Your Grace," Mrs. Dryden was saying testily. "There is no other option, for there is no cure for him!"

Lawrence looked at the embarrassed man and grinned. "Why don't you and your most excellent mother—"

"Oh, Your Grace!" Mrs. Dryden simpered.

Julia snorted.

"—return home," said Lawrence doggedly.

The three Drydens looked at him.

"Home?" repeated Donald.

"Home?" Julia stared.

Mrs. Dryden drew herself up. "I cannot permit my daughter to—"

"The trouble is, Mrs. Dryden, is that there are certain elements of the wedding that Miss Dryden and I must discus, and it simply cannot be done in your presence," Lawrence said smoothly, layering on the Penshaw charm as thick as he dared.

It appeared to have worked. Mrs. Dryden leaned forward curiously. "There is?"

Lawrence nodded sagely, then dropped his voice to a conspiratorial whisper. "Why, how am I supposed to concoct a surprise present for you, as a thank you for all the hard work you have put in to make this wedding a success...if you are here?"

A flush of pink, not unlike her daughter's, covered the older woman's cheeks. "Your Grace!"

"And so, if your son will accompany you," Lawrence said, rising suddenly, "I would be most grateful. I am sure you will be, too, in time."

It was well done. Within ten minutes—Mrs. Dryden thought it most important that he know just how mortified she was about Donald's tea incident, and how Lady Marnmouth would undoubtedly wish to hear about their ideas for the music—he had managed to bustle both mother and brother out of the room.

The door snapped shut. Silence reigned.

That was, until a heavy sigh from the sofa. "How on earth did you manage that?"

Lawrence grinned as he turned to Julia, dropping onto the sofa beside her. "I am not merely an excellent boxer, you know, but I have several years of training in the circles of the *ton*."

She giggled.

"Not much different, actually," Lawrence said with a chuckle. "Both packed full of vicious people only out to better themselves, both filled with gossip and slander, and both only have one victor at the end."

Julia's eyes sparkled. "And did you win?"

Lawrence answered that in the only way he knew how—with a kiss.

She gasped under him as Lawrence covered her with his body, his every inch—some inches more than others—crying out for her, but he would only permit himself a minute of frantic kissing before he pulled back.

Well. Maybe two. Three at the most.

When he finally released her and moved to the end of the sofa, Julia was panting, Lawrence was breathless, and he hardly knew what he was going to do with himself.

Have a very cold bath the moment she was gone. That seemed the only option.

"Oh, Lawrence," Julia breathed. "You make me feel—"

"I know," he said. "You can have no idea."

She breathed a laugh. "No, it's not just physical—though I admit, the physical part is wonderful. No, you make me feel...happy. Content. Joyful, safe, adored."

Lawrence's heart skipped a beat. How had he ever questioned if they were right for each other? How had Alan ever made him wonder whether Julia was working for Mortimer, of all things!

If it had not been for his cover, they would surely have found each other sooner.

But then, perhaps not. It was not something Lawrence thought too much on—the potential consequences were terrifying to the extreme—but it was possible, perhaps, that they could have met at Almack's, and...

Passed each other by. A lady with no title nor great fortune and a duke. There was no reason why they should have been introduced.

Lawrence shivered at the very thought.

"What's that for?"

He smiled at Julia's curious expression. "Just thinking what my life might have been like had we never met."

Her smile disappeared. "That sounds awful."

"Exactly," Lawrence said briskly. "And I have far more important things to consider. Just how many jewels I am going to shower you with, for example."

She snorted, Lawrence trying not to look at the way her breasts quivered at the movement. "Do not think of showering me with jewels!"

"You don't like diamonds?"

Julia turned, curling a leg onto the sofa so as to properly face him. "Do I look like the sort of woman easily impressed with diamonds?"

Lawrence arched an eyebrow. "You were impressed by my ability to knock a man unconscious."

"Precisely."

"You heathen."

Desire rushed through him as Julia leaned forward, her curves becoming all the more obvious. "Definitely."

Lawrence groaned. *How was a man supposed to stand it?* The tantalizing promise of pleasure was seated just before him, more and more of her breasts becoming visible with every inch more she leaned.

How could he distract himself?

"You mean to say that you don't want to be draped in pearls?"

Julia shook her head slowly, her gaze drifting from his face to his chest. "No, that's not what I want at this moment."

Lawrence swallowed, mouth dry. All he had heard about well-born ladies suffering through lovemaking were entirely untrue.

All the better for him, once they were married. But keeping his eagerness for her in check was getting harder with every passing moment. And that was not the only thing getting harder...

"You surprise me," he said aloud, trying to prolong the conversation on more sedate lines. "I know you did not fall in love with me knowing I was a duke, but I must admit, I thought you'd enjoy some part of it."

Julia halted, then leaned back. A strange expression flittered across her face, so swiftly Lawrence barely caught it. But it had been there, and it was…shame?

What on earth could Julia have to be ashamed of?

"I had avoided fortune hunters even when living under my name, and as mere Lawrence Madgwick, it was a little…freeing, I suppose, to merely meet people who could judge me for who I purported to be."

A small smile tilted Julia's lips. "Judge you by your cover."

"I suppose so." He grinned. "And here you are, unimpressed by the title, the wealth, the prestige—"

"It's not that I don't—I am sure I will adore being a duchess, your duchess," Julia said hastily. "It's more…well. My favorite memory of us is…"

Lawrence leaned forward himself now, his sleeve brushing past a cushion. "Yes?"

She looked down at her hands before replying with a nervous smile. "Eating those pies, sitting on the bank of the Thames."

For a moment, he just stared, delight sparking through his bones. Then Lawrence threw back his head and roared with laughter.

"Lawrence!"

"Well, it's just—"

"Your Grace?"

The door to the hall had opened, a footman standing there looking utterly perplexed.

Lawrence managed to control his laughter. *Well, this was an opportunity he could take advantage of, could he not?*

"All is well, Blenkinsop, all is well," he reassured the worried footman. "But please let it be known that Miss Dryden and I will be discussing something very grave and serious for the next…oh, next hour? And we are not to be disturbed—under any circumstances. You understand?"

Lawrence watched the footman's nervous gaze flicker from him to Julia, who was staring imperiously back.

God, he'd make her a duchess yet.

"Y-Yes, Your Grace," stammered Blenkinsop. "Not to be disturbed for an hour."

"At least an hour."

"Yes, Your Grace." The footman snapped the door behind him.

Julia was frowning. "A serious conversation?"

He nodded, not yet willing to let himself reveal all. After all, this had to be approached very carefully, did it not?

"You fell in love with me before you knew who I was," he said softly, reaching for her hand. Julia gave it willingly. "Before you knew what I could offer, when you thought you would be lowering yourself to become my wife."

Julia smiled gently. "And you fell in love with me knowing that. It's all a bit of a tangle, isn't it?"

Lawrence nodded, excitement rushing through him. "And you say your favorite memory together is eating the pies?"

She nodded, eyes bright. "Just talking and eating terribly good food, it really was criminal how good it was. The sunlight on the water, no one knowing where I was, no Mama trying to force me to marry some dolt..."

Her voice faded, and Lawrence's heart started pattering swiftly. *Yes, this was perfect. He would take advantage, by God.*

"Well, that is a real shame," he said with a mock sigh.

The light left Julia's eyes. "It is?"

Lawrence nodded seriously. "Yes. My favorite memory is when I ravished you so completely, you cried out my name in sweet ec—"

"Lawrence!"

Julia's cheeks were scarlet, her gaze darting to the door, but Lawrence saw no point in holding back. Not any longer.

They were alone, engaged to be married, and already knew the sweet delights of the pleasure they could share. *Why not have a little more?*

"Julia," Lawrence said quietly, creeping forward as Julia leaned back on the sofa with a growing smile, covering her body with hers. "I suppose we shall have to make some new memories."

"Oh, really?" Julia raised a quizzical eyebrow as her hands started untying the cravat around his neck. "You think you can do better?"

He could feel her heart quicken under him as her legs curled around him. Lawrence groaned, trying to focus, but tendrils of pleasure were already teasing around his thighs as he nestled between her.

"I think," he growled, kissing her neck and moving slowly up toward her mouth, "you are going to have to learn to be very quiet."

"No better time to start practicing," Julia gasped, capturing his lips with her own.

EPILOGUE

May 2, 1810

T HERE WERE FEW places Julia truly believed she did not belong. She had quite happily stepped into the Almonry Den what felt like a lifetime ago. Not once but twice had she stepped into an alleyway when, on the balance of probability, she should not have done.

But nowhere had felt so utterly intimidating as this.

A voice tutted behind her. "Do not tell me you are having second thoughts!"

Julia turned to her mother, who was wearing a resplendent new gown and a bonnet with more feathers in it than one bird surely contained.

She swallowed. "No?"

She was not having second thoughts, not exactly. *It was more...well.* Once she stepped across that threshold, everything would change. She did not want to go back on her word, but—

"Julia Dryden," said Mrs. Dryden sternly. "You love him?"

Julia blinked. "Of course, but—"

"You loved him long before you were engaged to him, didn't you?"

It was such an unusual sort of conversation with her mother, Julia hardly knew where to look. The trouble was, standing as they were right outside St. Swithuns, her in her wedding gown, the two of them receiving quite a significant amount of attention already.

"Yes," she said quietly, cheeks flushing under the thin lace veil her mother had declared "perfection" in Mr. Rivers' haberdashery. "Yes, I loved him before he proposed matrimony."

"Before you knew he was a duke?"

There was an arch look in her mother's eyes Julia had never seen before. The look one may give an equal, once that person had been found out in a rather clever subterfuge.

And Julia was wrong. Her cheeks could darken even further. "Mama, I—"

"I was always worried about you getting married, you know."

The words did not make sense. How could they? Julia had known her mother wished her to marry since the moment she had neared her entrance into Society.

"But you always—"

"Oh, I always, I always," Mrs. Dryden said, fussing with the cuff of her gown. "One day you will learn, my dear, when you have children of your own—" Julia's stomach jolted "—that there is nothing more wonderful than a daughter who knows her own mind, until she is yours."

A slow smile crept across Julia's face. "Truly?"

Her mother lifted her gaze and beamed at her child. "Truly. Now, am I going to be rid of you easily, or will I have to scandalize the whole of the *ton* and march you down that aisle?"

Though a small part of Julia wished she could see her mother do something so outrageous, she acquiesced to what was proper.

"No, you go inside Mama and take your seat. I shall be in directly."

Her mother fixed a stern look on her. "I should think so."

She bustled into the church.

Julia took a deep breath. What was it, holding her back? She loved

Lawrence, of that she was sure. She wanted to be his wife. Longed to be his wife.

Wanted to wake up every morning and enjoy the delights they had snatched in dark corners the last few weeks…

So what was so difficult about taking a step forward?

Organ music echoed through the air. The wedding march. It had begun, and all it needed was—

"There you are."

Julia smiled with relief as Donald appeared, offering his arm.

"May I?"

"I don't know," she teased as they crossed the threshold and into the cool of the church porch. "Have you any more objections to me marrying a boxer?"

Her brother winced as they stepped to the end of the nave, his whisper only for her ears. "You know perfectly well I would have never said that if I had known…"

Donald's words faded into obscurity as she glanced up and saw, waiting for her at the end of the aisle…

A tall man. Handsome. Dark. With hair that never seemed to stay tidy.

The Duke of Penshaw.

Julia took a step forward.

"Hang about, I'm meant to be taking you!"

Whether she took Donald or he took her, it did not really matter. All Julia cared about was the way Lawrence's gaze, the instant it met hers, quieted all fears and worries. How the frustrations of the past week became inconsequential, mere adventures to get her to here.

They had reached the front of the nave so swiftly, Julia hardly knew what was happening as her hand was removed from Donald's arm and placed on Lawrence's.

She looked up at him with wide eyes. "Lawrence—"

"Jules," he said with a gentle smile. "You look beautiful."

Heat seared her cheeks. "You have to say that."

"Probably," he murmured with a wry smile as the vicar started welcoming the congregation. "But that doesn't make it any less true."

"You don't look too shabby yourself," Julia whispered, looking him up and down appreciatively.

The fashionable breeches he now wore, in stark contrast to the loose ones he had worn as a boxer, gave a much better sense of the curve of his buttocks.

With horror, Julia tried to remind herself she should not be thinking such things at all, let alone in a church! At her own wedding!

Lawrence's fingers tightened on hers. "I know what you're thinking."

His voice was so low, she almost did not catch it—but her stomach flipped over as she did. "Lawrence!"

"You are thinking," he whispered quietly, "how much more pleasant it was at the Almonry Den where we could be ourselves, instead of standing here like statues with an audience."

Julia stifled a giggle. Glancing over her shoulder, she saw the church was indeed packed with those who looked as though rods had been shoved up their—

"—take this woman—"

Turning around hurriedly, Julia repeated the vows in a haze of excitement and affection. After all, had they not made more important vows to each other when wrapped in each other's arms? Were not the whispered promises made when making love far deeper than these?

"—pronounce you man and wife."

Julia blinked up at the man who had ceased to be her lover and was now her husband.

"You're my husband," she whispered, unable to help herself.

There was a twinkle in Lawrence's eye. "Whatever you say, Your Grace."

It was almost laughable. *Your Grace! What a thing to—*

Julia's smile faded as she and Lawrence were bid to sit down and hear the sermon. She was a duchess. The Duchess of Penshaw.

This thought crowded her mind so utterly, she was barely able to think of anything else until she was standing arm in arm with the man she loved in the impressive hallway where he had first revealed his true identity.

"Such a glorious wedding, I thought," boomed Lady Romeril, who had refused to take the delicate hint of a cough from a Penshaw footman and was entirely monopolizing them. "But then of course, the Duke of Penshaw was never going to stint on the details, was he?"

"I suppose not," Julia said weakly.

The Duke of Penshaw. She was married to the Duke of Penshaw.

Fingers tightened around her hand. She looked up into a handsome and smiling face.

Lawrence. That was who she had married. Lawrence, the boxer. Lawrence, the man who saved her. Lawrence, the man who loved her even though she was so far outside his social circles.

The painful pattering of fear faded away.

"—I said, do you not agree, Your Grace?"

Julia blinked. Lady Romeril was looking at her most sternly, though it appeared that was the only way she could look. "I beg your pardon?"

Lady Romeril sniffed. "You have much to learn about being a lady, if you ask me."

With a sweep of her skirts, she strode away.

Lawrence chuckled, immediately putting Julia's mind at rest. "Old baggage."

"Lawrence!"

"Well, she is," he said quietly, pulling her into the drawing room, which was quieter. "Goodness, I don't know what I was thinking permitting my sister to invite so many people."

Julia smiled weakly. Lawrence's sister was not someone she knew well, though she had seemed perfectly pleasant the handful of times they had met. "Well, you are a duke."

"Only on paper."

"The *ducal* deeds, yes," Julia teased as they stood beside a table covered in wedding presents.

Lawrence made a face that made her stomach twist with desire. *Oh, if only everyone could just leave...*

But then something strange caught her eye. "What is that?"

Lying there on the table, unwrapped and seemingly poorly made, was...

"Is that a horseshoe?" Julia asked curiously, leaning forward to pick it up.

It was indeed. Badly constructed, she could see that better now she was holding it. No horse would wear a shoe like this unless it was very unwell.

But for some reason, it caused a great smile on Lawrence's face. "Oh, how fantastic! It's from Dulverton!"

"Where?" Julia asked curiously, turning it over in her hands.

"Dulverton. The Duke of Dulverton. He's a...friend."

She raised an eyebrow as she handed the rather odd wedding gift to him. "Friend of the duke or friend of Lawrence?"

Her husband winked. "The duke, I'm afraid, but don't worry, he is...as accustomed to danger as I am."

Curiosity piqued, Julia leaned forward discreetly. "Really?"

Lawrence laughed. "Last I heard, he was on the hunt for someone rather particular."

"A blacksmith?"

"Sort of," he said evasively. "Now, don't ask me anymore, you know I cannot speak openly about these things."

It was most provoking, Julia thought as she took back the horseshoe, *but then, that was what came of marrying a duke in danger.* Lawrence was brave, braver than most. He had put his own safety on the line in the hope of finding a dangerous man—finding and capturing, which he had done.

She supposed she could let him have a few secrets. After all, she had one of her own…

"I promise I will tell you all about it, one day," Lawrence said, lifting a hand to cup her cheek. "I would never willingly keep anything from you, Jules, you know that."

Julia's heart sang. *Well, it had been a few months…there was surely no harm in telling him now…*

"Lawrence," she said quietly.

"Hmm?"

"I need to tell you something."

Lawrence's eyes sparkled. "Don't tell me that you're secretly a countess. Isn't it a little late for that?"

Julia smiled, excitement fizzing in her bones. "No, I am not a countess, I am a duchess. And he—or she—will be born with a title, unlike myself. I hope they are like you," she said wistfully, Lawrence's eyes widened in shock. "With my hair though, no offense."

Lawrence's jaw dropped. "No, you're not—you can't be—"

"At least two months gone," Julia confirmed sleepily, a smile dazzling across her face. "Though do not tell my mother, I will never hear the end of—"

Her husband crushed her into his arms none too gently, Julia thought with a laugh, considering her condition. "Oh, Julia!"

"Now, don't you get all excited," she said, throat choking with emotion. "I am more than enough excited for the both of us!"

Lawrence thrust her back, his hands on her shoulders, as his eyes searched hers. "But—oh, Jules, a baby!"

"A baby!"

They turned hurriedly as Mrs. Dryden screeched the words, dropping her glass of wine on the floor.

Julia groaned as the glass shattered and murmurs started up all around them. "That's done it. Anyone who can do the math—"

"I don't care," said Lawrence sharply, kissing her full on the mouth before pulling back and beaming. "And she can be anything she wants—"

"Or he," Julia reminded him as her mother starting sobbing hysterically on the other side of the room. "It could be a boy."

"Whatever they are," Lawrence said, eyes bright. "They will have the freedom to be anything!"

Julia's arm crept around her husband. "Anything? Even a boxer?"

He chuckled as he pressed his lips to her forehead. "Even that. As long as she takes lessons from me first. No daughter of mine is going into the ring without knowing everything I know."

Julia snorted, happiness pouring through her veins. "And then I'll take it from there."

About Emily E K Murdoch

If you love falling in love, then you've come to the right place.

I am a historian and writer and have a varied career to date: from examining medieval manuscripts to designing museum exhibitions, to working as a researcher for the BBC to working for the National Trust.

My books range from England 1050 to Texas 1848, and I can't wait for you to fall in love with my heroes and heroines!

Follow me on twitter and instagram @emilyekmurdoch, find me on facebook at facebook.com/theemilyekmurdoch, and read my blog at www.emilyekmurdoch.com.

Made in the USA
Monee, IL
20 January 2023

25132408R00128